I0822338

The Unblessed Witch

COPYRIGHT

Cover Designer – Tairelei – www.facebook.com/Tairelei/

Copy Editor – Second Pass Editing

CONTENT WARNING Violence, Language, Sexual Content, Death, ~~Ghosties~~ Spirits

ALSO BY MIRANDA LYN

FAE RISING:

BLOOD AND PROMISE

CHAOS AND DESTINY

FATE AND FLAME

TIDES AND RUIN

UNMARKED:

THE UNMARKED WITCH

THE UNBOUND WITCH

COMING SOON:

TIL DEATH

www.authormirandalyn.com

For those who know that love spells aren't the only kind of magic that can leave you spellbound and breathless.
And to those who don't know... It's books, okay? Books can also leave you spellbound and breathless.

What did you think we were talking about?
Getting railed on a sleigh ride?

Fine... it's that too.

FOREST
MOSS
RIVER
WHISPER
FIRE
MOON
STORM

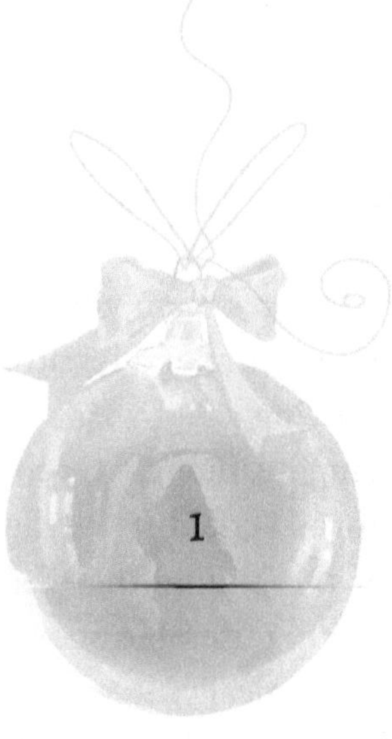

1

Snow was a thief of color. This blizzard was a thief of my sanity. Chunks of ice struck my frozen face, and wind lashed from all sides. No matter how many steps I managed through calf-deep snow, it felt as if I'd never reach the inside of the tavern drawing me in. Calling me like a ship's beacon.

Raising my shoulders to block the wind creeping around my neck and down my spine, I grumbled, squinting through Mother Nature's fury. I needed to see the world surrounding me to feel safe; to know that my stalker wasn't lurking nearby. I was the hunter and the hunted, as of late. Hazard of the job, though I hadn't seen him in months. But the storm raged on, and the power pulsing through my body became the overwhelming priority. I was going to burst soon, within hours likely, exposing everything if I wasn't fast enough, and the goddess would not approve of that. Because above all else, my spell was her secret. And my damnation.

I could feel him. My prey. A vigorous pull and a pulse of magic, urging me onward. Power swirled in my veins, pounding in a way I rarely felt. Ready. Eager to hunt down the goddess' next victim.

I'd been to the Fire Coven's main village before. Most hadn't. Few traveled to this conundrum of a territory. The easy mixture of witches and shifters living side by side unsettled most of this world. Things were changing, though. Or so we were told.

Still, through the storm, I couldn't see the closely built homes, the brick sidewalks, or the ground that had once been nothing but black ash. Only white, miserable snow and scattered street lamps with no glow. Technically, it wasn't nighttime yet, and, hopefully, the small blizzard would settle by then.

When I finally reached the tavern, I expected the door to be old and heavy. Shoving my body into it, seeking whatever meager warmth might be inside, it swung easily, throwing me forward. I slipped on the melted snow and would have crashed to the ground, had it not been for the mysterious man who caught me as if he'd been standing there waiting to rescue a stranger.

The second we collided, my magic threatened to burst. Snapping my mouth shut, as if my breath alone would expose me, I pushed the urge down as far as I could, praying to buy myself time. Of all the places to reveal myself, a tavern full of people staring would absolutely be the worst.

As I glanced into icy blue eyes, the left saved in spite of whatever caused the scar cutting this man's brow, something profound snapped between us. Something that made me buckle in a way I'd never known. His stare locked with mine, his stubble-covered jawline twitching. The smallest of indications but enough. He'd felt the magic, too.

I gasped as realization flittered over my sensitive skin. This was not a man. This was *the wolf.* Hand of the Dark King and legendary for losing his shifter ability trying to save our world. The ashy white hair framing his handsome face was a dead giveaway.

"I... uh..."

Words. What were words?

His sturdy arms didn't falter for a second as he brought me upright, our faces inches from each other.

Smoothing down the sleeves of my fur-lined coat, he stared down at me with a lopsided grin. "I promise there's nothing worth rushing in for, love."

Another swell of uncontrollable magic nearly burst from my fingertips. I gasped. It was him. The wolf was my target. That pulse was a warning, telling me not to trust the facade of this new witch. To let go of my control and release the power caged within me. But it was more than that. More than I'd ever experienced before. I stepped out of his arms and instantly felt the absence.

I needed composure immediately. I had a role to play, and I could not lose control. None of this had to be done publicly, and I could save us both from that, at the very least.

"Thank you... stranger."

"I'm nobody's stranger." He reached for my hand, brushing a thumb across the top of my knuckles as those eyes met mine again, his shoulder-length hair falling into his brow. "You can call me Atlas if you let me buy you a drink."

I wondered if he'd felt the electricity there. Too bad I'd been down this road before. Handsome man, full of charm, surface level, of course. Beneath, he was probably the worst kind of person. I knew his type. I hunted his type. I spent my life helping to change his type, but I couldn't fight the flush to my cheeks or the heat to my belly as I pulled back, shoving away the threat of exposure because I was weak, and this beautiful man took up so much space, tricking my mind into thinking we were alone.

"I'm not a drinker, but maybe something warm. Just this once."

Looking across the room, he called to the barkeep. "Something warm, Anna. For my new friend who doesn't have a name."

I had a name, of course, but I wouldn't offer it just yet. There was magic in the mystery. She flung a white cloth over her shoulder, smiling in a friendly way at Atlas before waving a hand. Her palm glowed orange as a steaming mug moved through the air and landed with a slosh upon an empty table on the far side of the room.

I pushed my hood down, revealing my thick red hair. If I were home in the Storm Coven, it might have been my calling card. But here, I was an outsider. Atlas shuffled back, his shock as his eyes fell down my curls nearly stole my breath, though I didn't understand the reason behind it.

Emotional sensing, True Sight. Another spell I'd received. I could cast upon anyone, and tell you how they were truly feeling, if I wanted. And, sometimes, when I didn't want to. But more than that, the goddess had decided, when I was seventeen, that it wasn't enough of a burden for a witch, and so I'd received the magic of the Heart Seeker. Power that made me the huntsman of lost witches' fates.

Atlas turned to walk away.

"You're not joining me?" I asked, knowing I didn't have a lot of time.

Running his fingers through his hair, he flashed a smile and shook his head. "Maybe next time."

I should have tried to coax him outside. Especially with the magic pushing on my insides, eager to be released. I could nearly hear his name, coated in power, coursing through my mind. But curiosity got the better of me, and instead, I crossed the busy room, squeezing past other patrons crowding their tables, to take a lone seat in the corner, half-covered in shadows. It was drafty, but Anna's tea was warm and calming.

The door slammed open again, flurries rushing inside as another colossal man, similar in stature to Atlas, stomped in, kicking the snow from his hefty boots before puffing breaths of air into his brown hands. Draped in thick fur pelts that broadened his massive shoulders, he could have been mistaken for a baby giant if I hadn't already known him to be *the strix*.

"Cold as a witch's nipple out there, huh, Tor?"

I hid my smile, lifting the hot tea to my lips and blowing the steam away as I watched the man swipe the coils of his dark brown hair covered in ice and plant himself at Atlas' table near the door. The barkeep didn't need an order from him. The mug was waiting by the time he scooted in his chair and reached into his pocket, pulling out a few coins.

I nearly choked when a piece of burning, black parchment drifted down from the ceiling, landing on the table before Atlas. He shot a wary glance at his friend before lifting the paper to read the message.

Atlas furrowed his scarred brow as the message turned to ash. "Aw. Come on. Can't someone else do this?"

The other man's low voice was alluring. Deep in a soothing way. "Everyone knows you're avoiding magic, Atty. He says you can do it the old-fashioned way. Go on foot."

Atlas' eyes narrowed before he lifted his cup. "The old-fashioned way is gone. A foot is hardly a replacement for a paw. We both know I'll never run as a wolf again."

I didn't need magic to pick up on the sadness, the utter devastation of those words. Still, the room's cacophony hid his friend's response; the volume returned to a normal degree as the rest of the witches and shifters returned to their conversations, and these men did the same.

Time passed with easy giggles from the surrounding tables as Atlas entertained those around him. Though, the strix checked the door far more than his friend seemed to realize.

I'd spent a lot of time lurking in crowds and hiding amongst strangers. If not to escape the man that hunted me, then simply to do my job. It was nothing to sit in a room and take in a crowd, reading each person as if their lives, emotions, histories were written like novels, translated into their mannerisms and hidden feelings. Everyone wore a mask; some were just better at the camouflage.

When Atlas laughed, his gaze would cut across the tavern to me. And fuck, I couldn't keep my eyes off the man. I recognized his brokenness. More than those around him likely, but there was something else there. The victims of my magic were typically growly and miserable and nothing I told them came as a shock, but that wasn't the case for Atlas. There was joy and genuine happiness, if not a sliver of desperation to keep his friend's attention.

Below all of that, though, as I slowly pushed power through him, reading him and releasing some of the building tension within me, I felt the damning gash in a way I rarely did. Atlas was scarred beyond the physical mark that cut down his forehead and through his brow.

The small bit of sun illuminating the frosted windows had long since faded when the man that used to be the strix shifter stood heavily from the table, clamping a hand down on Atlas' shoulder. "Another time, my friend. This old man is tired."

And he was tired, but he was also not being fully honest. There was sadness in those words, too, even if he didn't say it aloud. His heavy retreating footfalls were hardly audible as the patrons, far more drunk than when I arrived, grew louder.

Sweat formed on my brow, fingers trembling as I continued to push away the threat of exposure. I wouldn't be able to sustain much longer. I'd either have to coax Atlas out of the tavern or somehow cause a distraction while warning him, hoping I didn't glow like a beacon in the night when I lost control.

A wave of loneliness crashed over me as the door snapped shut. *Atlas.* I didn't have to look to know he was watching me. I could feel him. And I wanted his attention, though I shouldn't. I tried to convince myself it was part of the role I played as I unbuttoned my coat with shaking hands and nodded again to Anna, who sent a fresh cup of steaming tea.

Before I could draw him in, someone else sat down at his table. The beautiful witch easily enraptured him as he shared the same friendly smile he had with me. Still, as she ran lithe fingers over his chest, leaning in to whisper, I couldn't help the ping of jealousy. Which was completely out of line and absolutely a problem.

This was simply a job. I would have my moment with him, one way or another, and then I'd never have to see him again. I had to be close but not seen. Which was mostly fine, except he was so nice to look at.

"I wouldn't bother with that one." Anna had crossed the room to wipe a table behind me, and I hadn't even noticed. "He'll come home with you, for sure. Just won't be there in the morning."

Wringing my hands below the table to stay the pressure, I forced a smile. "Fear of commitment, huh? I know the type."

She snorted. "Not like this one. The wretched ones are easily forgotten. Atty's lovable."

"It's fine. He's not my type."

She leaned over my table, looking at me with a grin. "I'd believe you if you'd taken your eyes off of him for more than thirty seconds since you got here."

"I'm not… It's not… I'm working."

"Not my job to judge you; only warn you," she said, throwing her hand towel over her shoulder and walking away.

"Imagine if you had to do both," I grumbled, reaching for my tea as I twisted in my chair, determined to look anywhere but at Atlas and the woman practically crawling onto his lap.

Disgusting.

I counted. Actually fucking counted up to five minutes in my head, staring at the floor, the door, the snow blowing so hard outside it looked like a white sheet covering the window, lit behind by the moon.

There was absolutely no way I was going to get away with doing this discreetly. Too many people, too little space. I convinced myself the strange draw to him was the blizzard outside, amplifying my Storm Coven power. He wasn't special. He wasn't even that handsome. His laugh was irritating.

The heavy groan from a chair sliding across from me caught me off guard. I glanced up to those eyes that might have been my undoing if the situation had been different. Maybe it was self-preservation. The power jolted within me, and I gripped the edges of the table to steady myself. He had no idea who he was approaching.

"You never told me your name, Frostbite."

"You never asked."

He smirked. "My mistake. Mind if I sit?"

My heart thundering in my chest might have betrayed me if he'd still had wolf ears. I absentmindedly checked the door out of habit.

"The company is not so alluring on this side of the room, but if you insist."

"And the name?"

"It's uh… Marley."

"Marley. I like it."

Speaking my name like a song, he flipped the chair backwards and plopped down, folding his arms over the back as he tilted his head to Anna. She winked and, within seconds, sent a tankard our way. He had drunk only a little, I'd noticed. He seemed to be here for the camaraderie more than the festivities. Most of the marks I met in taverns were hopeless drunks with horrid lifetime trauma and hardly any desire to heal from it. For the first time, I was glad someone worthy, or so it seemed, might be saved from themselves. If he was smart enough to listen to the Spirits.

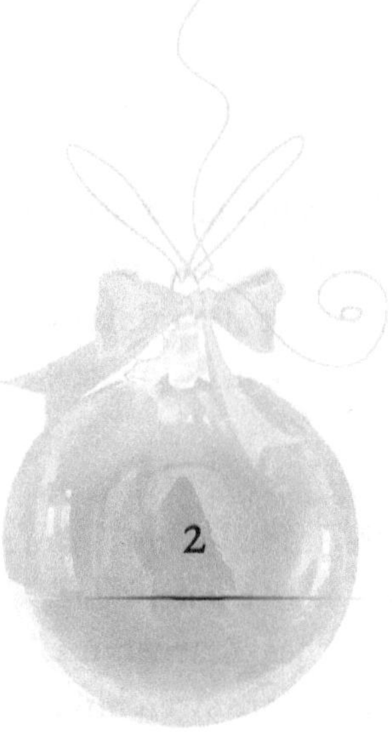

"Storm Coven, huh? I would have guessed Forest."

I sipped my tea, staring at the man like a fool, trying not to blush from having his undivided attention. He must have smelled my coven on me like an animal."Why?"

His eyes sparkled with mischief as he replied. "Because you're far too pretty and not dressed for a blizzard like a Storm Coven witch would have known to expect. You should have felt it in the air long before it hit."

"So, you think Storm Coven witches are all hags? I travel a lot. The weather doesn't really bother me."

Atlas laughed so hard he nearly fell out of his chair. The room silenced at the beautiful sound, though it confused me.

"Why is that funny?"

How could a man with a laugh like that be so broken?

I pushed magic forward, letting it encircle that deep, dark place in his heart to remind myself that he was. And this was a job, nothing more. I'd deliver a message coated in power tonight, and that would be the end of it. I only hoped the surging magic would let it happen on my terms.

He leaned forward, wrapping his arms around the back of the chair, showing off his muscles as he raised an eyebrow. "You were blue for the first twenty minutes today. I had to keep watching just to make sure you didn't keel over."

"Hardy har, Wolf."

He jerked upright, his gaze sharpening.

"I'm right, aren't I? 'Animal scent'? You're the one who used to be a wolf, and now, you're a witch?"

"I'm still a wolf at heart, trust me." He leaned forward, checking my empty cup before stretching.

The door creaked open again, and I couldn't help the falter in my heartbeat as fear jolted through me. I lived on the edge of anticipation. Waiting for Levin to find me as if he lurked around every corner. Usually, the fear was worse than the man, but after several near-death experiences, it was warranted.

Atlas followed my line of sight, waving to the woman that entered before asking, "Another?"

"I think that's plenty of tea for one evening. At this rate, I'll be up all night."

He wiggled his eyebrows, raising his drink. "You know, I hear that's not always a bad thing."

I believed he meant to unnerve me, but I simply stooped to his level. "Only heard? Never experienced? That's a shame."

He choked on his drink, and I met his stare, daring him to respond. That flutter in my chest was new, though. I wasn't sure if it was from the challenge in his eyes or the way my body sizzled in response to his steamy gaze. He leaned halfway across the small table between us, and I moved in as if he'd lured me on silent command.

Thick fingers traced my jawline, but he did not speak a word. He stared so hard, the rest of the room seemed to melt away. Atlas could have demanded the world in that moment, and I might have given it to him. Catered to my baser needs. But ultimately, this was why I was here. Only lust filled that gaze, and though my heart raced, especially when his eyes dipped lower, I knew better than to get tangled up with this damaged man. His jaw dropped when I broke the spell between us and slumped back into my chair.

"I still have to find the inn."

Clearing his throat, he said, "There are two in this territory. I'd recommend old Enger's place. It's in the square right across from the market. Can't miss it if you go left down the main road."

I brushed my thumb over my lips, staring up at him through my lashes. I needed to get him out of this place. "It would be even easier if a handsome stranger wanted to help me find it."

The words were like fire in my throat, sealing his fate as I invited him to be alone with me. I almost felt bad for the poor soul.

"Stranger, huh?" He leaned back again, scanning the faces in the room. "Plenty of those here, but handsome is asking a lot. Oh! How about that guy over there? He's pretty handsome."

I laughed, reaching for the coat over the back of my chair as I glanced up at the mirror Atlas had pointed to. "He'll do. Make sure he doesn't get handsy."

"No promises. They say he's a scoundrel."

"Maybe that's how I like them," I said, narrowing my eyes.

He patted his pocket. "I have a weapon, just in case you get any ideas."

My cheeks flushed. I had plenty of ideas for his weapon, and none of them were decent.

He pushed the tavern door open, snow pelting me in the face, and dropped a heavy fur over my shoulders before taking my hand to lead me through the blizzard. The second our fingers touched, that same jolt of electricity surged through my body like a lightning storm, threatening to take over my waning control.

Shit. I'd have to do this soon.

Within minutes, we had trudged through the snow to a little place in the town square. The building was easy enough to see in the dying storm as most of the windows had glowing candles on the sills. Somewhere, beyond the whistle of the wind, there was soft music playing.

Atlas twisted the handle, dragging me inside, and turning to look down at me, his face lit by candlelight. As if by instinct alone, as if he could not help himself, he stepped so close I could count his thick black lashes.

Two freezing palms caressed my cheeks as he used his thumbs to wipe beneath my eyes. "You're covered in snowflakes, Frostbite."

I grabbed his wrists, wanting so badly to haul him to the room I hadn't yet secured, while also wishing I could push him out the door, saving him from this fate, even if it was ultimately supposed to help him. Magic pulsed, a hair's breadth from release, within my veins. My control over the spell was nearly gone, and I wanted nothing more than to curse the goddess for the intrusion.

A small door had been left ajar, and heavy footsteps drew near. I needed to decide quickly. Did I push my luck with Atlas, drawing out this moment between us, or do my job and lie low? To remind myself that this was not real, and he didn't truly want more than a single night with me, I stroked my power again, feeling only lust. And, damn, if it didn't ignite my body, warming me to the core as I melted.

"You could stay," I whispered, ignoring the desperate tone in my voice.

"That's a dangerous invitation, Marley."

I could see it then, the desire within his eyes, biting his lip as if he needed to decide to be chivalrous or the scoundrel he'd promised.

I moved to my tiptoes as he leaned down. My lashes, wet with snow, brushed my cheeks as I anticipated those beautiful lips.

His hands tightened on my face, tilting it ever so slightly as that bead of passion erupted.

There was not a deep well of feelings for me, and I didn't expect there to be. I knew what I had signed on for the second he took my hand. But morally, how far could I let this go? Could I have him and damn him on the same night? Every inch of my body said yes.

Full, smooth lips devoured mine until I couldn't breathe, couldn't think beyond the man that had consumed me the second I'd been close enough to feel this power between us. But just as soon as I thought I could get lost in him, a throat cleared in the background, wrenching us both back to reality.

"Atlas," a masculine voice boomed.

He didn't step away from me, didn't even take those hands from my cheeks, or his eyes from mine as he smiled. "Got a room for a pretty witch, Enger?"

A blush creeped across my face as I stepped away and turned to face the innkeeper.

The stout man crossed his arms over his chest. "Would that be a room for the pretty witch or a room for the pretty witch and her incorrigible friend?"

"The night is young. Let's not make hasty decisions, Eng."

Before I could get a single word in, Enger lifted an iron key from a hook behind the counter and tossed it to Atlas.

"The cauldron room. You know the drill."

"Up the stairs and to the right. Got it."

"I think that should be a red flag, Wolf," I said the second I was sure we were out of earshot of the innkeeper.

"It definitely should be." Atlas gave me a lopsided grin before shoving the key into the lock and twisting.

As we stepped into the room, the fireplace surged to life. Shifting closer, I held my hands out to warm them as the wooden floor creaked beneath my steps. It wasn't a massive room by any means, but there was a level of comfort in the simple furnishings covered in busy floral print.

"Let me ask you something," Atlas said as the door clicked behind him. "You traveled here but didn't secure a place to sleep. You are clearly staying at least one night, but you don't have a single bag with you. You watch the door as closely as you study a room. What are you here for?"

The magic surged faster than I could have been prepared for. Doubling over, I stepped away from the fire, pushing it down, urging it to let me have control.

He had to ask. He had to fucking ask. And the magic knew. Like a being, pacing and waiting until it was called forward.

Atlas stepped toward me, reaching as if he could help. But it wasn't me that needed help.

"Holy shit, Marley. Your eyes are glowing."

He stumbled backward, knocking a lamp to the floor before slamming into the door.

A voice that was not my own ripped from me as I lifted from the ground, the magic fully consuming me. "Atlas Firepelt, you have been marked by the goddess for change."

"This is not exactly what I had in mind, Frostbite. What's going on? Actually, no, scratch that. I don't want to know. I take back my questions."

The power could not hear him.

"Listen carefully, witch. On three of the next five nights, upon the stroke of midnight, three Spirits will visit you. Past, Present, and Future will damn your soul to eternity if you choose to keep your heart sealed from this world. This is your only chance for salvation. Heed this warning and be wary."

The echo of a threat rattled around the room as the magic vanished, leaving a terrified man standing at the door, and me, sullen and sorry.

Atlas held up a shaking hand between us, as if he could build a wall there. "What the fuck was that?"

I moved to him, but he jerked his head backward, repulsed.

Studying the grain within the planks of the floor, refusing to look at his face, I whispered, "You will not allow yourself to love another, though you have a heart worthy of it. The goddess has selected you for redemption or disaster. Something… someone… is going to come to you at night. You'll understand then. What you need to do to save yourself."

"This is… You're wrong. I'm fine."

My chest tightened. "Atlas, please listen."

"No. You just stay the hell away from me."

He yanked the door open and stormed out of the room, leaving me standing with my head hanging. It was always the same. Denial. But as the clock struck eleven, I silently wished him well, knowing I would probably never see that beautiful face again.

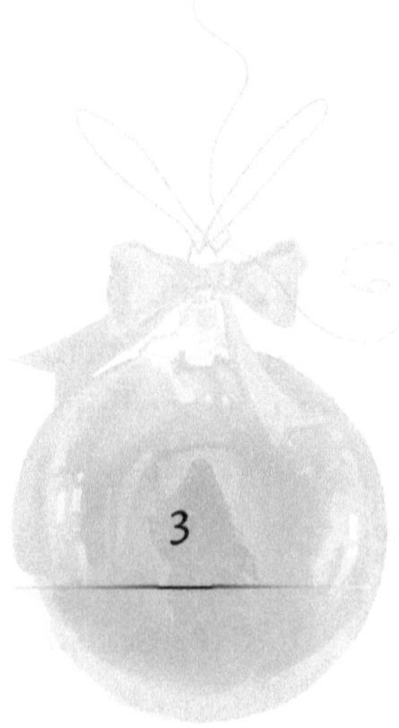

3

Three ghostly, hooded figures lingered above my bed, bony translucent fingers protruding from threadbare, graying robes as they pointed at me in unison. All three choosing to be hidden within the shadows of their oversized hoods.

"You called?" Present asked, her voice like sharpened gravel.

"Almost an hour ago," I grumbled, peeling down the blankets on the bed, so I could finally crawl inside. "Nice of you to promptly answer."

"You should have more fear, Marley Stormborn." Past moved to the sweeping curtains, staring up at the clear night sky.

I cut a glance to Future, the only one of them I would ever hold my tongue for. If not for the ominous shadows that billowed beneath her, then perhaps because I'd never seen her eyes, and there was always danger behind the mysteries of this world.

Noticing my wary glance, Past laughed, the sound like fingernails scraping down a schoolhouse chalkboard. "There is fear in this one, Future. You just have to know how to see it."

"He's been warned," I said, ignoring them. "The magic has begun. He has five days."

"We've been doing this for longer than you've been alive, girl. We're perfectly aware of how many days there are until Solstice."

"Great. I'm tired. Go teach your lessons. But be nice to this one. There's goodness in him."

Future swooped closer, hovering above my nose as I looked up into the void where her face should have been. I flinched, and my heart stopped as she spoke. "There's goodness in all of them, dear. Otherwise, they would never get a choice."

I swallowed, remembering strong hands wrapped around my throat, eager to take my life. "There is nothing good in Levin Riverden. I can promise you that."

Past swooped in, half of her body disappearing as her shoulders aligned with Future. "Ah. But there used to be."

The last word echoed off the walls as the three identical figures vanished. I thought of Atlas as I crawled into bed. Of the look in his horrified eyes when he saw the magic. Of the disbelief of his own soul.

But that was the point. He didn't know how broken he really was. None of them did.

I lay, tossing and turning as I listened to the soft crackle of the fire, watching the shadows it cast dance in the room and along the walls. He could get through this, I reminded myself as, finally, my eyes grew heavy and drifted shut.

"WHAT THE... WHERE AM I?" I WHISPERED, STARING AT PAST AS she looked onward, eyes locked on a figure snoring in a bed that was nearly too small.

"It begins." She pointed a long, thin finger at the sleeping man.

"No," I gasped. "I'm not supposed to be here. That's not how this works. I warn them and stay close. This is your job. Send me back."

Past's head snapped toward me as she rushed forward, causing me to stumble backwards. "Do not deign to tell me what my job is. You are here because the goddess wills it. You are nothing more than a pawn in her games. Just like the rest of us. Lose your attitude, and be silent."

I swallowed the lump in my throat and said no more as I took in the room. A pile of clothes tossed into a corner made my stomach turn. He'd been wearing them tonight, though they smelled more of ale than they had when he'd left me. Otherwise, the small space was tidy. I peeked out the window, taking in nothing but snow illuminated by the sea of stars above, smothering the world.

"Wake up, you big oaf," Past screeched, waving a hand to rip Atlas' blankets from his naked body.

His glorious, naked body.

I gasped and turned, covering my eyes with my hands as the beautiful image of that man burned into my memory. The moon had lit all the right places, and I heard a moan that could have been my undoing. He still hadn't woken. Not until there was an enormous thump, and the walls faded to nothing.

When I turned around, the bed had disappeared, but the naked man remained, standing in all his glory. Atlas's locked eyes with mine, daring me to let my gaze wander. I jumped and spun again, but not before I noted the simmering anger on his face.

"This is not real," he said, the sleep still heavy in his voice. "Leave me alone."

"This is real, Atlas Firepelt," Past hissed. "And if you do not stand and dress, you will come on this journey naked. You are quite nice to look at, so I bestow upon you your first gift of choice."

"I don't take orders from ghosties."

Past's voice grew in volume, the sweetness melting into something sinister. "I am not a ghost. Or a wraith. I am a Spirit. Selected by the goddess herself. I have power, boy. Do not insult me again, or it will be your last."

Loud footsteps crossed the room, but I kept my back to him, my face buried. I wanted nothing more than to be a million miles away from him right now.

He mumbled to himself. "Pork? Did I have pork yesterday? Maybe it wasn't fully cooked. That's what this is. A bit of undigested food, come back to haunt me. Maybe it was ale. Or the rum. Might've been the rum—"

"Will you be speaking to yourself this entire time or eventually shutting up? I do hate it when everything starts in denial," Past said, putting the bed back in place as the floor became engulfed in shadow.

"Marley?"

I turned to face him, slightly disappointed to see he'd pulled on trousers and was shoving his arms into his coat.

"I'm sorry," was all I could manage. And I was, though I knew deep down it was for the best. This would not be a tranquil night for him.

"Then make it stop," he demanded, stomping over to stand before me.

"I can't. It's not me. I am just the Heart Seeker and messenger. My power is only to find you and call the Spirits of Solstice Past, Present, and Future. The rest is up to you."

The room had nearly faded to black, the planks of the wooden floor and pile of clothing, the only things remaining. Atlas turned in several circles, likely working the magic out in his mind.

Eventually, he said, "Tell me why you're here."

Lowering my voice, I inched backward. "I don't know. I've never seen this part."

Past swayed back and forth as she removed her hood, revealing the striking face of the new queen.

"Raven? What the hell?"

"It's a trick. Past will always take the face of someone you know." I glared at the Spirit. "She's annoying like that."

"But aren't I so pretty with black hair?"

"Stunning," I answered, hoping the sarcasm was clear. But as she giggled and circled the room, I wondered if she'd heard of the word before. I tugged on Atlas' arm. "We're going back to see—"

"This is not your lesson to teach, Marley." Past whipped around, muzzling me with her magic. "Be silent."

I threw my hands in the air, glaring until the spell was released. "Fine. Let me go. He doesn't need me to be here for this. It's only going to make it worse."

Atlas grabbed my hand, the trace of worry in his voice jarring. "What are we doing?"

"She cannot say, but you'll see."

The whistling of the wind swept through the room until nothing beyond the horrid noise could be heard. Snow whipped and fell, turning the world white. Atlas yanked me to him, muscular arms wrapped around me as he tucked his face to brace for the storm. The last sound we heard was Past's cackle as everything faded to peaceful silence.

"Please don't do anything to make me hate you," Atlas whispered into my ear before stepping away.

The memory unfolded, appearing like a winter painting around us. The rocky ground and mountainside gave a familiar view: the Moss Coven. Several lines of tiny, green canvas tents tied down with cords of rope hid within the growing banks of snow.

"Can you hear them?" Past asked, a giggle in her voice as she clapped her hands, excited for the misery she was yet to bestow.

A chorus of youthful voices grew from barely a sound to

shouts of excitement as a crowd of children neared us, emerging from the tree line like a pack of wild animals. Atlas whipped around, his eyes wide as he finally realized what this magical curse would be.

"I remember this place," he said. "I remember this."

Walking forward, he bent to peek into a tent, its door flapping in the wind. Looking back at me, he grinned. A genuine, boyish smile. "This isn't so bad. Is this it then, Past? You're going to show me some childhood memories and sing campfire songs with us?"

"It's not that simple," I warned.

The children, not yet teens, surrounded us in a circle. Past had selected her spot perfectly. Radiant faces grew in anticipation when they swung their arms over their neighbor's shoulders and swayed back and forth, a single motion.

"All in," the smallest boy shouted.

"All out," the rest answered, including Atlas, who'd returned to my side.

"Watch," he whispered, pointing to the only dark brown tent.

As if on cue, the flap flew open, and Torryn, though much younger, stepped out. His long twists of hair were tied back with a piece of leather, shoulders covered in layers of mismatched furs, similar to how I'd seen him before. He pulled on the hand of a boy, yanking him from the tent before he knotted the door shut once more.

Atlas whispered, "That's me."

I knew. Those eyes were unique to only him. It was strange, though, seeing that ashy white hair, messy and wild on a boy so young. I wondered if it was the wolf peeking through.

"Line up!" Torryn shouted.

The children broke apart like tiny soldiers, moving into a shoulder-to-shoulder line across the tiny camp.

"As you know, it's almost Solstice."

There was a small shuffle amongst the children, but mostly,

they kept their chins high, and their feet planted as they listened to the young instructor. "Every year, the shifters go home for Solstice. You get three days off this mountain before you return to your training."

Beside me, Atlas seemed to shrink. His shoulders slumped, head bent forward, shaking from side to side as he moaned. "Don't do it, Tor."

The memory froze as Past grew to three times her normal size. "They cannot hear you. They cannot see you. They cannot even feel your presence. We are not here to change the past. Only to remember."

"Can you stop with the creepy thing? And you couldn't have picked a different time? This is… not my favorite. How about when I dove off a cliff even though no one else would? That's a glorious memory."

"This is exactly the right one," she snapped, moving down the line of children while returning to a normal size. "I'll stand over here beside our fearless king." She clasped her hands in front of herself, batting her eyes at a raven-haired little boy, as if she were truly the queen and madly in love.

"There's something seriously wrong with you," I said before turning back to Torryn.

"For sure," Atlas agreed.

Torryn's smooth voice rang through the mountainside. "Atlas won't be returning home. His father has decided he should stay for extra training during Solstice break."

The white-haired boy cast his eyes to the ground, deflating with fists clenched at his side. Out of curiosity, I used magic, slipping my hand behind my back so grown-Atlas would not see the glow from the marking. Reading his face only, I would have guessed fury coursed through his veins, but no. It was dejection. And humiliation. Even as a child, he masked his feelings well. I stepped closer to the man beside me, if for no reason than to assure him he was not alone.

He didn't notice, though; hadn't taken his eyes off that sullen little boy.

"Who is always the first to enter the training circle and the last to leave?" Torryn asked, watching each boy's face.

"Atlas," they answered.

"And who was the first to volunteer for watch by himself in the woods?"

"Atlas."

A taller boy with messy blond hair shouted above whatever their instructor had planned to say next. "And who gave me his supper when mine fell in the dirt?"

A few of the boys laughed before answering. "Atlas."

"And who promised to show us where the girls' camp is?" another shouted.

"Atlas," Torryn yelled, more power in his voice than before.

The little white-haired boy's cheeks turned red before shrugging.

Shaking his head, the little king yelled. "Raise your hand if you would like to return home and leave your shift-mate on the side of this mountain by himself over break."

None of the children moved. Not a single damn one of them. I could have cried for them all. For the surge of pride I'd felt for a group of youthful souls I'd never even met. Because in their silent conviction, they reminded me so much of my little brother. From his messy hair to his toothless smile, he was there. Blending into Atlas' memory as if it were my own. Though mine had met with a tragic end. One I could not find the courage to deal with.

Young-Atlas finally raised his head, staring into the faces of each one of those stoic children who would not let him suffer a holiday alone.

"You can go," he said, tears pooling in his eyes. "You can go see your families. I'll be fine here by myself."

"Not on your life, Atty," the little king, then only a prince, said, stepping out of line to bump shoulders with his friend. "All in. All out."

"All in. All out," the others yelled, filling the silence.

The memory faded away like a dwindling fire, leaving us standing in the same spot, though the children had all disappeared, and the moon shone down. I swallowed the lump in my throat, never realizing how moved I'd be by someone else's history. The deep roots of where this man had come from went far beyond the comforts of a shifter's home.

"Watch," Past said, pointing toward the tent closest to us.

Though intrigued, I knew my presence here was invasive and wrong. My toes curled as I caught Atlas staring at me. I'd sooner crawl out of my own skin than intentionally invade his memory like this. But I had been forced into this place, just as he had, and I hoped he knew that.

Two boys emerged: the little king and another with chestnut hair and big brown eyes, rimmed with tears.

"But I'll miss my mom," the boy cried.

Bastian wrapped an arm over the boy's shoulder, leading him purposefully away from the tents as he whispered, "It's not about what you'll miss. It's about what you'll give by choosing to stay. We're all going to miss our families. But we'll have each other."

Atlas stepped closer to the boys, looking back at me and then at the children again. "This isn't a memory. I don't remember this."

Past swooped forward, an unearthly smile on a face that wasn't hers. "No one said I had to use *your* memories."

With a tick in his jaw, Atlas turned back.

"What if it were you? What if your father said you couldn't come home? Would you want to be stuck up here all by yourself?" Bastian asked.

"My father would never turn me out."

"Why didn't you raise your hand?" Atlas ran his fingers through his hair, dropping to a knee before the boys. His voice softened as if the child he'd once been had spoken, instead of the towering man.

"You could have raised your hand and gone home," Bastian said, shoving his hands into his pockets.

"I don't want to leave Atty by himself. I don't want to miss Solstice, but I wouldn't want him to be alone."

"That's the spirit," the young king said, clapping the boy on his back. "It'll be fun. We'll make it fun."

Again, the world shifted. Daytime with Torryn overlooking all the boys, minus Atlas.

"He'll be done soon. He bathes faster than all of you. Tie your knots. Quickly," young-Torryn said.

The children chattered, rushing through the final knots on whatever craft they were making. A small white wolf emerged from the tree line, holding a towel clenched between his teeth. I gasped. Even as a pup, he was stunning. Hair nearly fading into the banks of snow surrounding him. Regal and mischievous. I stumbled forward, enraptured by the beauty of the little beast. Atlas rose, eyes locked on his former self. Excitement grew on the faces of the little ones as they packed in tight, hiding what they'd been working on behind their backs.

"Off to dress now, Atty. Be quick about it. We've got chores, and you're falling behind."

The wolf sprinted into a tent and emerged a dressed boy in just a few minutes. His shift-mates had wrapped their project in brown paper, and I couldn't help my smile as I watched grown-Atlas' face looking down at all the children that must have had such a special impact on his life.

"We made you something," Bastian said, stepping away from the group.

"It's a blanket," another shouted, too excited to hold in the surprise for a second longer.

"Why?" that innocent little voice asked.

"Because when we go home, we will all have a Solstice gift

waiting. And just because your dad's a prick, doesn't mean you don't deserve one, too."

The rest of the kids snickered, but Torryn cleared his throat. "Your highness?"

Bastian turned, swiping black hair from his face. "What? I didn't lie, did I?"

"Watch his eyes," Atlas whispered from beside me, jutting his chin toward Torryn. "There, did you see it?"

I should have told him I could feel the pride. I didn't need to see it, but I didn't bother. Instead, I shared a smile with the broken soul and left it.

As the vision melted, Atlas turned to Past. "Okay, this isn't so bad. For a punishment."

I held my breath as she crept across the space, staring at him with preternatural stillness. "This was not your lesson, boy. This was only the starting point of your loneliness."

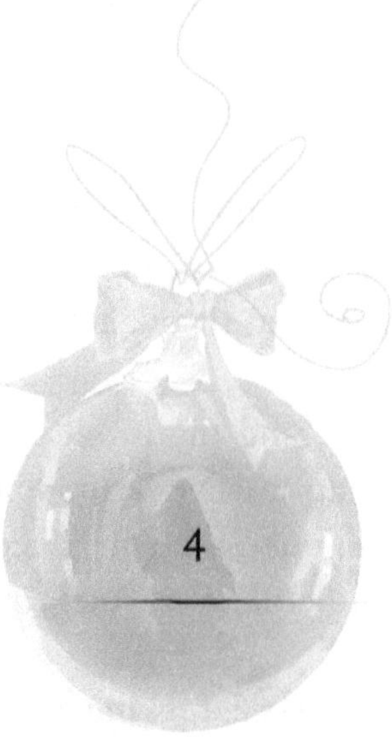

4

Breathing became a chore as I watched Atlas' face turn from annoyed acceptance to utter disbelief when a log cabin appeared around us. The round wooden planks forming the walls held no dust, and the floors covered in faded rugs were spotless. A calming sense of someone's warm home settled over me, nestled within the careful folds of the blanket hanging over a rocking chair and the smell of freshly baked bread. Atlas spun, running for the door, but his hands passed through the knob. I wished that escape for him more than he did, I thought. But there would be no ending to this. Not until Past had taught her lesson.

"I can't be here," he murmured. "This… Not here."

The door slammed open, flying through him as if he were a wraith, and a younger version of him stepped into the small cabin. "Mother? I'm home."

"Back here, Atty," a sweet voice called. "Stomp the snow from those boots before you traipse it through my house."

"I remember this day, too," Atlas said, studying the pelt of a bear that his teenage form had dropped onto the table near the door. “Don’t do it.” He stormed across the room, stopping in front of younger Atlas. “He won’t feel pride. Walk away.”

As the young man passed through Atlas, his handsome face fell.

Past waved her hand, and the room transformed again. An older woman with beautiful silver hair down to her waist and eyes that matched her son’s stood in a bedroom, cleaning the window. Her features lit with joy as young-Atlas walked in.

“I’ve done it, Mother.”

“Have you now?” she asked, tucking a cloth into her apron as she looked up at her son. “What are we celebrating?”

“I found the perfect Solstice gift for Father. I did all the hunting and pelt work myself.”

“Atlas—”

“He’s been extra hard on me lately, and I know it’s because he thinks I can’t do these things. But I can prove it to him now. He’ll be proud. I promise.”

Grown-Atlas moved toward me. I snatched his hand that shook with fear as his potent emotions overwhelmed me. Something haunting crossed his mother’s face like a shadow, and that was enough for me to hold on tight when the door slammed open again, and Atlas flinched.

“Can I give it to him now?”

“It’s a few days early. You should wait, Atty.”

“What’s this?” A booming voice asked from the front of the house.

My heart raced as Past squealed. Though my magic didn’t work on her, the excitement was disgustingly palpable. I’d never known how cruel the Spirits could be until this moment. Perhaps Future was right, and I should have had more trepidation.

Deep, measured breaths caused Atlas’ shoulders to rise and fall from beside me as he prepared himself for what he knew was coming. Each blink was deliberate, each swallow the same as tension grew static in the humble home.

Young-Atlas snapped his fingers. "I accidentally left it by the door."

"Well, then. Let's go see what he has to say," his mother answered, failing to hide the worry in her tone.

We followed the memories back to the front of the house where a man with a striking resemblance to his son, though he had green eyes and a crooked nose, stood holding the bear pelt.

"Happy Solstice, Father," young-Atlas said, his voice deeper than it had been, holding out a hand to shake his father's. "I did it myself. Every part."

The man looked down to his son's outstretched hand, ignoring it as he held the lush brown fur up to examine the work. He studied the edges of the pelt. Atlas, still clutching my palm, had looked away, focusing on his mother's face. He gulped as his father shoved the gift at young-Atlas.

"He's only twelve, Bjorn."

The man closed the distance between himself and his son, clasping his shoulder as he pushed him toward the door. "Get out."

"What?" young-Atlas protested, trying to tug himself from his father's firm grasp. "It's just a gift, Father. I don't understand."

"You can hunt. You can feed yourself. You can provide your own clothing and shelter. Leave now. And if you ever return, I'll kill you."

My gasp was smothered by his mother's heart wrenching scream.

"Bjorn!"

When his father returned to the cabin moments after expelling his son, shoulder's heaving as he slammed the door shut, Atlas' mother launched herself at him, fighting and pushing and screaming to get to the door.

"Make him come back, Bjorn. You make him come back."

"It doesn't work that way," he shouted, grabbing the woman by her arms and holding her away. "Stop this nonsense. He is a wolf. A good wolf. He's started his training. He will be fine."

She broke, crumbling to the ground. "I need him. I just need him a little longer."

"One day, when he is a man and has a pack of his own, we will find him again. And we will see what kind of man he's grown to be."

"He will be nothing but hateful and broken, Bjorn. I do not choose this. I do not want this for our son."

A breath, nearly inaudible, rattled beside me. "He thought I was a threat to him. As wolf shifters, he was the Alpha. He had no choice." The words were like a mechanical reading. As if he'd said them to himself repeatedly throughout his lifetime.

The room froze as Past appeared in front of us, taking on the face of Atlas' distraught mother. I'd forgotten she was there at all as the horrific memory played before us.

"So young," she said, her voice changing to mimic the woman. "You never saw her again, did you?"

He blinked, a single tear trekking down his face. I hated this. Hated it for him and for me. In some ways, I was glad to be here to see the hell I initiated for people, but I fucking hated that I was the pawn for this. Hated that I caused this misery.

"You are not the cause," Past whispered into my ear. "You are just a tool."

"I couldn't go back," Atlas murmured. "I tried. My father hired a guard and forced me to stay away. I was young and alone, and he was doing what he thought was best for me. But she never chose this. And all this time, I thought she had."

I squeezed his trembling hand. "No one could choose to leave you. I'm sure of it."

"Please don't use that face," he begged Past. "Anyone but hers."

A wretched smile peeked through as she swirled and changed

into a beautiful witch with several clear markings and hair nearly identical to mine.

"No!" Atlas gasped, dropping my hand as he fell to his knees. "Just kill me and be done with this."

The world around us faded away. The last thing we saw was that young man walking alone into the forest beyond.

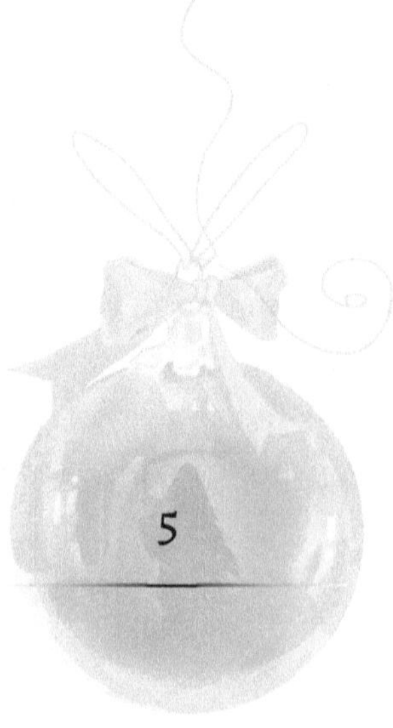

A frozen lake with thick fog nestled above the ice that appeared around us. For several moments, Atlas still on his knees, I wondered if anything would happen at all.

"If you have any sort of mercy or power over this," he said to me, face buried in his giant hands, "You will not take this a second further."

"Your demands will go unanswered in this realm, Atlas Firepelt. She has less control than you do."

He rubbed his chest in circles, likely trying to soothe the bitterness that grew with his realization. Every limb in my body grew in weight until I wished the world would crack apart and swallow me whole. The heaviness of regret sitting upon my shoulders was as familiar to me as breathing, but still, I would never grow accustomed to it.

I swallowed the lump in my throat. "I'm sorry."

"I can't do this. I won't do this."

"You must," Past insisted from somewhere out of view.

Four young women, bundled in long coats and hats that hung low on their heads, finally appeared. I saw that fiery red hair before I even heard their voices. Heard the moan from Atlas' lips that wracked me with despair.

"Please," he whispered. This time not to me, or even Past, but to the goddess herself as he stared up into the heavens, pleading with someone I knew wouldn't answer.

"Please," I repeated, not realizing the word sat on my lips until it was audible.

But the unanswered prayer was lost between this realm and that of the past as the girls walked directly through us, heading toward the lake.

"This is foolish." One of them took the hat from her head. "One day, you'll get us all killed, Laramie Forestbrook."

"Not this day" the redhead dropped her coat to the ground and stepped naked onto the ice.

"You're sure this is going to work?" another said, shivering as she too removed her cloak and bared herself for all the world to see.

"Gilly Forestburn said her grandmother walked naked across this lake and met the love of her life the very next night. They haven't spent a day apart since. And if Gilly Forestburn is a goddamn liar, then I'll punch her right in the nose."

Even in his despair, Atlas couldn't help the huff of a laugh at the young woman's conviction. He moved to his feet but, this time, did not come near me. Instead, his eyes remained glued to the naked redhead, forcing her friends to walk across a frozen lake in the dead of winter.

Envy seeped into my veins as he stared at a woman that had clearly left him broken in a way he would never recover from. Would she have changed this moment if she'd known what was to come? Would he?

As the women, trembling and turning blue, made it to nearly the halfway point, a group of young men ran into the clearing, whooping and hollering as they hoisted Atlas above their shoulders. I recognized the king's cousin, Grey, amongst them and Torryn trailing in the back.

The men fell to silence, staring dumbfounded for several long moments. It was Atlas that finally rolled from their grips to surge forward and gather the coats in his arms, flashing the men behind him an ornery grin as he brought his fingers to his lips. His eyebrow had a minor cut, but nothing of note, compared to the scar he had now.

"Atlas, don't," Torryn warned, golden eyes fixed on the tree line in the distance, refusing to look at the naked women. "It's cold as a witch's nipples out here."

"At least as cold as theirs." He laughed, rejoining the shifters.

"Hey," Laramie shouted, finally realizing the men stood on the bank. "Drop those coats, or I'll make you all wish you were never born."

"I've never been scared of a witch, and I have no intentions of changing that today, woman," Atlas yelled.

"Then you haven't met the right witch," another of the girls called, trying to cover her bare body with her hands.

Not Laramie, though. She stormed across that lake, each step a stomp, as if daring the ice to betray her. Confident and mad as hell, she jumped onto the frozen grass and moved to stand before the boys, hands on her hips.

"Look away, boys," Atlas said, eyes wide. "I think I'm about to fall in love."

She didn't hesitate, not for one iota of a second. Hauling back, she balled a heavy fist and punched Atlas square in the nose, practically breathing fire as she yanked the coats from his hands and spun, marching back with just as much conviction as she'd come with.

"Holy shit." Young-Atlas hadn't taken his eyes from the girl.

"Somebody catch me," grown-Atlas said the same time as his younger self. "I've already fallen."

"What's your name?" he shouted through the fog.

"Go to hell," she screamed back.

The men laughed as the memory faded away.

"Prepare yourself," Past whispered into my ear.

I wasn't ready. Not to watch him fall in love, be in love, or break. I didn't want to do it anymore, and I didn't know what was coming.

My heart ached for Atlas more than anything as a bridge appeared beneath us. Past was nowhere to be seen as two people raced down the road, laughing and holding hands as they neared.

Younger-Atlas captured Laramie in his arms and swung her around, the love between them so apparent, I didn't have to use my power to know anything more about these two young, carefree souls. A shifter and a witch.

"I got you something," the woman said, reaching into her pocket as they stepped onto the bridge. "For Solstice."

His eyes were sparkling, drowning in adoration as he stared at her. A lovesick pup, if ever I'd seen one. "I got you something, too."

She swatted his arm. "I told you not to. I know times are tough."

"It's nothing much." He shrugged, reaching into his pocket. He plucked a small vial of water from within and held it out to her. "A year ago today, you punched me right in the nose and changed my life forever. I know I haven't said it yet, but I've loved you from that very second to this one. Every minute. I've lost sleep thinking of you. I've forgotten meals, worried about you. And I know it's difficult, us sneaking around so you don't get caught with me. But I wouldn't change it for the world, Laramie. You are everything I don't deserve, and someday, witches be damned, I'm going to marry you."

"I love you, too," she said, gripping the vial as she tossed her hands around his neck, red hair swinging when he lifted her and spun once more.

I had to look anywhere but at the man that had kissed me

only hours ago, even if his memory couldn't see me, and the real version hadn't so much as glanced my way. Whatever that tiny spark might have been between us last night was, it wasn't this. This was raw and pure and the closest thing to perfection I'd ever seen. I was only an intruder of their perfect memories.

"But what is it?" Laramie asked moments later, staring through the glass vial.

I began walking. I could not be a part of this anymore. But no matter how big of a step I took, no matter which way I tried to go, I never moved from my spot beside the lovers. Clamping my eyes shut, I rebelled against Past's rules.

"You must watch, Marley." Past appeared beside me, still in the form of the beautiful witch young-Atlas clung to.

His voice was so full of hope and happiness. "That day at the lake, I knew one day it would be you and I against the world. I knew I'd never stop until we were together, no matter the obstacles. So, I chipped a piece of ice from the lake and kept it."

"This entire time?"

"I know it's not much."

"Atty, no. It's perfect. I wish I could stay and show you how much I—"

A sharp gasp cut through the cold, forcing my eyes open, and I spun just in time to see the stricken look on both of Atlas' faces. Blood dripped from Laramie's nose and then her ears.

"Past," Atlas screamed. "Enough. It's enough."

My mouth fell open. The Harrowing. Goddess be damned. The fiery witch with the purest love hadn't betrayed him. No. No. No. This was so much worse.

"Laramie?" Young-Atlas' voice broke into a thousand pieces as he reached for his witch, carefully taking her face into his hands as he searched her vacant eyes for an explanation.

Atlas moved to my side, shoving his fingers into his hair as he spun around, refusing to watch, trying and failing to take in a breath. I wanted to help him, to console him, but what could I do that would fix this? There was nothing. So, I rested a shaking hand on his back and moved it in slow circles as young-Atlas panicked and lifted that poor cursed witch into his arms.

"Tell me what to do, Lar. Just tell me what to do. Laramie!"

My legs fell weak, pressure building in my chest because I'd forgotten to breathe. The devastation was monumental. Tears filled my eyes until I could hardly see through them. I couldn't think past the swell that grew like a dagger in my throat as Atlas silently cried beside me.

The scene changed, yanking us into the center of the Forest Coven's main village, swarming with witches.

"No. Atlas, no." My eyes widened. "Why would you bring her here?"

"I thought…" he answered from some place far, far away, though he remained beside me. "I didn't know how else to save her."

The screams from the witches came first. But young-Atlas shouted above the crowd. "Please. There's something wrong. I don't know what happened."

"What have you done?" a woman shrieked, breaking through the people to stand before the shifter. "What have you done to my daughter?"

"I don't… I didn't. Please, she needs help right now."

Though Laramie had gone rigid in Atlas's arms, a man covered in markings yanked her away. The second he took her, Atlas took three steps back, showing his palms. "Please. We love each other. I don't want any problems."

"You cannot love a witch, you disgusting animal. You are incapable," someone from the crowd yelled as they cast, sweeping Atlas's feet out from under him as he crashed face first into the ground, landing on the sharp edge of a rock the size of his own boot. Blood poured from his forehead rapidly enough to pool below him as they pinned him down with magic.

"You will watch the pain you have caused her," Xena

Foresthale, the Forest Coven leader, said, yanking Atlas' bloodied face from the ground.

He squeezed his eyes shut, either to block out the world or to keep them from filling with the blood from his wound.

Laramie lifted from the ground, her arms outstretched, head fallen back at an unnatural angle. There would be no saving this witch. Only one had ever survived.

"Please," Atlas begged from beside me. "Make it stop."

It was as if he'd counted. Replayed this memory in his mind so many times, he could recite the exact seconds of her death. With his back still turned, facing away from the memory, he reached for my hand, trembling. I moved to stand before him, wrapping my arms around his waist as that body, no longer caging the wild soul of that witch, fell to the ground with a thud.

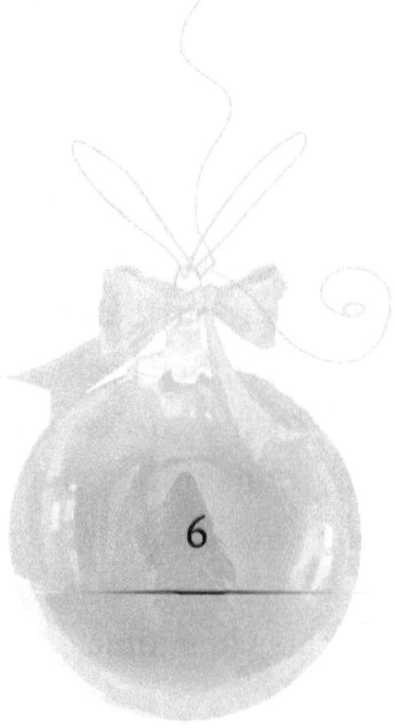

6

"I know you're in there, Marley!"

The angry shouting from outside my room yanked me from sleep. The sun had barely inched above the horizon, casting the room in deep amber shadows. I jerked upward, forgetting where I was for only seconds, until that rough voice yelled again.

"Open this fucking door."

Ripping off the blankets that had tangled my legs, I stopped for a second, wrapping my robe and tying it around my waist. Of course he would have questions. They always did, but typically I didn't answer the door or let them know where I was staying. Last night was different, though. As today would be.

Twisting the handle with a firing heartbeat, I was not shocked to find him just as disheveled as me, one arm holding him against the doorframe, the other mid-knock.

"I'm fairly certain there are other people trying to sleep here, Atlas."

"Oh yeah? Like I was last night before your ghosty wrenched me out of bed and put me through hell?"

I couldn't answer that. It was a fair question and obviously rhetorical. Instead, I reached forward, grabbing his loose collar, and dragged him into the room before quietly shutting the door. He moved swiftly, striding back and forth for several minutes, fingers twined in his coarse, ashy hair. He'd pause, open his mouth to say something, and then return to his pacing, nearly stumbling over the boot strings he hadn't bothered to tie.

"Have you been here the whole time?" he finally asked. "Here, as in sleeping in this room."

"In a sense, but if you're asking if I was with you last night, the answer is yes. I think I was."

He moved to a chair and flopped down, hunching over as he looked up at me with sullen eyes. "The last time I asked you a question, magic took over. A type of power like I've never seen. Am I going to cause that again? Will questions provoke some other curse?"

"No."

"Then explain it to me."

I took the chair on the opposite side of the fireplace, now full of only cherry hot coals, not a single log left to burn. "How far back do you want me to go?"

"As far as it takes to make this make sense. What is your power?"

"Like any witch, I have several. But specifically, there are two that are required to begin this… curse, as you called it. True Sight tells me how someone is feeling, the depth of their soul without having to ask. But it goes beyond that. Because I am the Heart Seeker, I can detect the blackness. The symbol that indicates they need somebody to intervene and aid them."

"So, what happened? I ran into you last night by happenstance, and you just decided I would be the perfect little candidate for your power?"

I shifted backward in my chair, looking out the frosted

window into the lilac-painted sky, wondering how the world could be so beautiful and yet so terribly cruel.

"It's not that simple. There's a tie between the goddess and I. She blessed me when I was just a child. Came to me in the dead of night, proclaiming I was to be her Heart Seeker. Before every Winter Solstice, I hunt those that are the most lost and call upon her Spirits to help the witches see her generosity."

He grimaced. "I've seen some pretty fucked up shit in this word, darling. I can promise you, I am not the worst of the worst."

"It's not about being a terrible person. The worst people are already damned. She believes this to be salvation. And I don't choose the targets. The power within led me to you." I stood, becoming uncomfortable with talking so openly about my magic. "I've seen shitty people, too, Atlas. People that I didn't believe deserved the goddess' mercy."

"This is not a mercy. It's torture. This is living in every moment that's haunted me since they happened. This is taking a knife and shoving it into an old scar, just to see if it will still bleed."

Placing my warm palm on the window, I turned my back to him, letting the cold seep into my skin. To remind myself that this world was far greater than the tension in this room. Perhaps he would kill me. "I know it feels that way, but—"

"No. Don't defend this. Unless we have evening plans to dive into your worst memories, you don't get to tell me what this is supposed to feel like."

My hand collapsed to my side. "You're right. I'm sorry."

"Call them."

I jerked around. "What?"

He stood, planting his feet. "You said you could call upon her Spirits… call them. Here. Now."

"Trust me, you do not want me to do that. You'll meet them soon enough."

He crossed the room to take my hands. "I don't want this. I didn't ask for any of it. Your magic is wrong. My heart is not marked. Broken things are never put back together without flaws, Marley. The damage will always be visible if you're willing to look hard enough. I am the same as everyone else."

I pulled my hand away to place it on his chest, pushing the magic forward so that I could feel that mark, reassure myself I hadn't gotten the wrong man. But as that link between us tightened, electrifying my touch, I yanked it away, staring up into his eyes and whispering, "It is there, Atlas. And I'm so sorry for it."

He ground his teeth together, fury turning his face into something that might have been terrifying had I not already cared for his soul. "Call. Them."

"You're not ready. The three Spirits are Past, Present, and Future. If at any point, Future thinks you're unsalvageable, it's over. You will wander this world alone for the rest of your life, and there is nothing anyone can do about it."

"I've got news for you, darling. I've been alone for most of my life."

I pressed myself forward, grabbing his collar so he could not look away. "You are not alone beyond anything but your own choice and perspective, and therein lies the fucking problem. I've dealt with many witches. It's not always love and fear of commitment. Sometimes, it's obsession with worldly things, sometimes, it's people that will not let go of a grudge that has festered so long, it's hurting others. Sometimes, it's a mother grieving from child loss. Or a father, wondering how on earth he will raise his children without his wife."

"How does it end?" he asked, eyes glancing between mine as if I held his fate within the answer.

Time slowed as his conviction wavered, albeit still swirling with anger, and another emotion came through. The lust I'd seen from him the night before. And though I felt him trying to shove it away, being this close made it nearly impossible. His tongue darted over his lips. A betrayal of his intended fury.

"It always ends with a choice," I managed, utterly captivated by him. "You can either choose to heal and move forward, or you can continue on your path and damn yourself. Unless..." I faltered when his throat bobbed, nearly losing all thoughts.

"Unless?" he whispered.

"Future decides you are not worthy of the choice."

"Fine." He grabbed the hand on his chest and yanked my body flush to his. "I've decided I'm healed. That's my choice. If I was so broken, how could I look at you and want you as much as I do?"

His lips collided with mine. He hurried his hands into my hair, and I moaned. Melting below the desire pulsing from him. It took everything in my power to push him away. To see within his heart that he didn't mean a single word he said.

"I saw the way you looked at her last night. You're trying to bury that pain. I think that's what you keep doing, what you've done for all these years. It won't change the mark, Atlas. It only proves the point."

"The attraction between us is real. You and I both know that," he said, inching forward.

I tried to think outside of myself, but I could not. That pulse was so strong, I nearly swayed as he grabbed me again, tucking a lock of hair behind my ear, his finger brushing my jaw.

His voice turned husky. "Let me show you that I am not broken." He smoothed a thumb over my bottom lip, licking his own. "Let me show you that I am free of my past."

My ears rang with the ache of passion, my body surging to life with every touch. His massive hands roamed my body as he asked, in so few words, for permission to show me how perfect and whole he was.

"This is a bad idea."

"I don't care," he said, resting his forehead on mine. "I'm full of those."

"Atlas..."

"Do not say my name like that and expect me to be decent, Frostbite. Maybe I have a lesson to teach you as well."

The promise of pleasure in those icy features was all I could think about as I reached for him. Perhaps this was why I was broken, too. I knew the feelings of the man and didn't seem to care that he'd just been emotionally destroyed. This wasn't about me. Not in this moment, and probably not the next. But selfishly, I needed him to touch me. To satisfy that pulse, that draw that did not falter. If only to walk away at the end of this with no regrets.

He bit my lip, a roguish smile burying everything else, his perfect facade. Something in that prick of pain mixed with the way his hands tugged at the knot tied at my waist, his knuckles brushing my stomach, lit me on fire. But also riddled me with guilt. Could I do this? Become the bandage to his misery?

Determination crossed his face as his eyebrows knit together, and he took a step forward. Goddess, it was hard to say no to this man. Especially as he backed me against the wall, caging me between his arms.

Staring down at me, his chest heaved, a question within his gaze. He would let this be my choice, even though it was his personal balm. It wasn't about the woman, only the release. The reminder that there was still pleasure in small moments. But I'd never be her. And I couldn't look at myself in the mirror if I let him continue to bury his feelings.

I shook my head, ducking under his arms to step away.

"I will call them," I whispered, watching his muscled back as he pressed his forehead to the wall, catching his breath and nodding.

We both knew it would have been a mistake.

Seconds passed. He collected himself, and maybe I did the same, preparing my heart for whatever might happen. He turned to face me, leaning back against the wall before looking up at the water stains on the ceiling.

"Before you call them, what's the worst that can happen?"

"Future is the final decision maker. If you say something wrong and she decides we cannot save you, she will use the power of the goddess to damn you on the spot. Your friends will leave you. You'll never be able to grow close to someone again."

"There's not enough power in this world to take my friends from me. I do not fear her."

I stepped forward, resting my palm on his chest again, feeling the racing heart below. "It doesn't matter if you fear her or not."

"Then call them," he said, lowering his chin as a shadow crossed his features.

I stepped back, facing away so he could not see the worry and sadness. With a power that burned as much as when the goddess touched my face, I called upon her magical Spirits.

"They don't always answer right away. You might as well get comfortable."

His eyes roved over me once before gripping the handle of the door. "I'll go find some breakfast. And unless you want to kill me slowly, Frostbite, get dressed."

"Any other day, and I might have enjoyed that," I teased, the sadness of the decisions made this morning still hanging in the air.

I'd just finished fastening the last button on my shirt when he knocked on the door, far more gentle than the wake up call. Still, I jumped. Anticipating the Spirits always left me on edge.

Despite walking in balancing a tray of options, he managed to catch my glance as I peeked down the hallway before shutting the door. Our eyes met for a split second, but he said nothing about it.

"Where did that dress come from? You didn't have any bags last night."

"I did. You just didn't see them." I waved a hand over the robe

I'd been wearing and let him watch as it shrank to almost nothing. "It's not really a spell that will win me any battles, but it's useful for my job."

"And here I get to conjure spiders and run a little faster than everyone else."

"It's not really... It's not normal to tell people which spells you have, you know."

He lifted a shoulder. "You told me."

True. I'd been far more open with him than any other marks. But then, none of them had made sure I had a warm bed in the middle of a blizzard. I'd never been a part of their journey. There had been no pull in the past once I'd called the Spirits.

Atlas slathered a knife full of butter across a thick slice of bread and shoved half into his mouth. I had no clue how he could make such a mundane task look so seductive, but there we were.

I poured two cups of tea, handing one to him before sitting in one of the floral printed chairs by the hearth.

"How long did you say this could take?" he asked after the food was gone and he'd fixed the fire.

"It's never been more than an hour. But I've also never called them in the middle of a job."

"I see." He peeked at the clock hanging slightly crooked on the wall.

"Do you have a hot date to get to?"

Snorting, he shook his head. "No. I've got to leave for a few days. Do something for Bash."

His words washed over me as my delicate teacup fell to the floor and shattered. I jumped to my feet. "Leave? You cannot leave."

"As a grown man, I can assure you, I'm perfectly capable," he said, crouching to pick up the larger pieces of porcelain.

"No, no. It's not that. It's just that... we have to stay together. Until... it's done."

He froze, eyeing me suspiciously. "What do you mean?"

"I'm the anchor for the Spirits. I have to stay close, or they cannot find you."

He clapped his hands together, startling me. "Well then, that's the answer to all my problems. I'll just leave, and you stay. Then they can't find me, and it'll be over."

"No, Atlas. If the Spirits cannot find your soul, they will call Death to find it."

"How do you know?"

"Because the very first marked soul I ever damned was my brother's. And when he ran away while I was sleeping in the room next to him, the Spirits made me watch as Death dragged him off to hell."

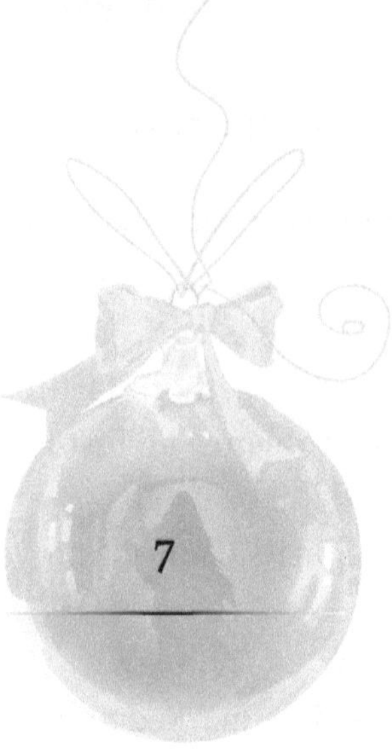

7

"What do you mean 'come with you?'"

Dropping the last pieces of the broken teacup into the small bin beside the door, I turned to face the man that was quickly becoming a pain in my ass. Wrecking my emotions and turning everything that had become routine upside down.

"Bash is making me gather the Yule logs from the covens. I have to have them here by the night of the Solstice celebration."

"Well, you're going to have to tell him you can't do it."

He crossed his thick arms over his broad chest, looking down his nose at me. "So, let me get this straight. You're telling me, if I go and you don't, I'll die. Dragged off to hell by Death himself. Oh! And I also have to live through the most painful moments of my life again while you stand back and watch. And I find myself at the mercy of some ghosty named Future. I also have a choice in none of this, but you absolutely refuse to come with me for the one job I've been given for the entire holiday season because you 'don't want to'. Even though you spend your time traveling the coven territories, anyway. Does that about sum it up?"

I raised an eyebrow. "Look. I don't know you. I'm trying to do my part, but there's no way I'm throwing myself at the feet of your good pal, the Dark King, and his magical doors, knowing he could just lock me up somewhere and I'd never be seen again."

"Listen, sweetheart. You had no problem with this stranger when I was kissing you. And he's not the monster people say he is. You saw him in my memories. Did he give off dark and murderous intentions when he calmed that boy? Also, who said anything about using him? I only travel by magic when I have to."

"There's no way we can walk to the other six covens before Solstice."

"So, you're coming. Great."

"You are infuriatingly stubborn, Atlas."

"It's a gift from the goddess."

"I think I hate you right now."

He feigned shock, pressing a hand to his chest. "I've never had a single person in my whole life hate me. How will I ever survive it?"

I scowled. "Something tells me you'll manage."

Just to spite him, I used magic to pack the extra blankets and pillows he'd requested after we gave up on waiting for the Spirits to come.

"A sleigh? You want to take a sleigh?"

"Isn't she a beauty?" Flashing his lopsided grin at me, he slammed a hand on the door.

Parked outside of the inn, the sleigh took up most of the snow-covered road. The sun beamed off the jagged icicles hanging from the buildings, daylight filling every crevice of the land. The Fire Coven came alive, witches and shifters scooping the remnants of the storm from their homes' steps and walks, some gathering to watch the giant carriage.

"We're absolutely going to freeze to death, and none of this will matter."

"Not exactly, Frostbite."

He pointed to a marking on his arm and squeezed his eyes shut, peeking once. When nothing happened, he cleared his throat and repeated the process. The spell lit blue, and he waved his hand, making a giant glass dome appear, enclosing the sleigh. When he felt my stare, he adjusted his sleeves and glanced away. "Still working on the casting part, but hey, I made a door this time."

"I thought you said you could conjure spiders and run faster. You said nothing about this."

"If I had listed everything, it would have been bragging, and no one likes a showoff."

"And you've never been a showoff a day in your life, I'm sure."

He stepped forward, grabbing my waist and hoisting me into the sleigh with ease. "Not one."

For a moment, as the reins cracked through the chilly air and the team of huge, black horses tore off, gliding across the top of the snow, I let myself believe in the beauty of it all. I hadn't enjoyed Winter Solstice since I'd met the goddess and damned my own brother. But only a fool could deny the vision of perfection painted across the world. Hues of lilac never left the sky, though it mixed with tones of gray from smoky chimneys. Giant flakes of snow fell, their descent slow, dancing along the breeze that carried them over the silent world.

"We just need to make one quick stop before we go," Atlas said, pulling the reins that seemed to float through the magical glass he'd conjured.

I said nothing, tugging the hat on my head a little further down. Atlas reached below the seat, lifting a giant bear fur, not unlike the one he'd made his father. Dropping it across our laps, he shouted at the horses, and they turned on command. Pine trees came and went as we covered ground, headed straight for a gleaming white castle that could have easily been lost in the blanket of snow.

My ears rang as we neared the Dark King's castle. No longer the small child from Atlas' past, but a man with a history as violent and threatening as any witch that had ever been born.

I grabbed Atlas' hand beneath the fur. "Why are we going there?"

"You'll see," he said, excitement lighting his eyes.

When we approached the gate, they opened with a groan, and the sleigh soared right through, stopping in front of the largest set of doors I'd ever laid eyes on.

"Do you want to come in?" Atlas asked softly.

"I'll wait here, if it's all the same to you. I'm sure they're lovely. But I'll pass."

I didn't miss the look on his face as he hopped out and sprinted into the castle. When he returned with a woman in tow, I nearly fell over myself trying to stand quickly in the sleigh.

"Your Highness," I said, curtsying as best as I could as she approached the door. "I would have gotten out. Atlas didn't say what we'd stopped for."

"Don't be silly. It's freezing out here."

The queen's dark curls blew across her face as she turned to Atlas, swatting him on the arm. "You did that to her on purpose, didn't you?"

"Absolutely."

"I don't think you've brought someone back to the castle since I've been here," she said slowly, eyes flashing between us.

"We're not staying," we said in unison.

"Just needed this one favor," he continued. "It's for Solstice after all."

"The doors would be so much faster, Atty."

He hung an arm over her shoulder. "Why use magic when you have the world at your fingertips?"

She shoved him away with a smile. "Some people would kill for your power."

"And some have killed because of it," he answered without missing a beat.

Her blue eyes flashed to me. "Good luck with this one. Maybe try to convince him that magic, in all forms, is a blessing." The queen with no markings cast before me and, had I not been staring at her, I might not have believed it. Because she was unmarked, but also because I'd heard she'd lost her power, saving us all from the old coven leaders.

A small but radiant ball of fire appeared, suspended in the air at the front of the glass dome. Everything instantly warmed as the heat went directly to my bones. I couldn't help the sigh.

"Well then," she said kindly. "Enjoy your trip."

"Thanks, Rave."

She reached for her friend, pulling him into a hug and whispering something into his ear before dipping her chin to me and rushing back inside. Two men carrying boxes walked out of those great doors, and Atlas helped tie them to the rear before hopping into the carriage and shutting the door with his magic.

"You could have warned me," I said, nudging him with my shoulder as he took his seat.

"Where's the fun in that?"

The uncomfortable silence grew between us, as it so often did with strangers. He'd been so lighthearted and free this morning. I didn't know how to go back to the heavy questions swirling through my mind. Eventually, I had to say something to fill the quiet. But before I could form words, he beat me to it.

"What's your favorite color?"

"All the questions in the world, and that's what you want to know?"

"It seemed the safest to ask."

I rubbed my fingers through the fur on my lap. "Blue."

"It's going to be a long journey if we only sit in silence," he said, vocalizing my thoughts. "We should make a game of it. You ask a question, and then I will."

"Do we get to pass if we don't want to answer?"

He lifted an eyebrow, staring down at me. "No. I'm nosy."

"And unaware of boundaries?"

"You scared to reveal yourself to someone the goddess believes is broken, Frostbite?"

"No," I lied.

"It won't matter anyway, Marley. As soon as Future comes, we can go our separate ways and be two people that went through something together."

"Okay, fine. Why are you afraid of using magic?"

A tiny vein showed in his forehead. "I'm not afraid."

"So, we're lying when it's convenient for avoidance. Got it."

"No. It's not fear, really. It's just..." He scratched his head. "I don't want to rely on something I could lose. Being the wolf was my entire personality for a long time after my parents kicked me out. There was solace there. A sense of happiness. I learned how to just... be. I learned how to run and hunt. How to live. And now it's all gone. To be honest, I don't want to be a witch. I won't lie about that. But it's far more stubborn nature and mourning than it is fear. I miss the wolf and the freedom he gave me."

His answer shocked me. Placing a bit of the puzzle in place, I thought I could step back and really see the man for more than his captivating smile.

"My turn." He adjusted himself on the bench, shifting to face me a little better. "What marked your brother's heart?"

I was not prepared for that question.

My expression must have surprised him because he wiggled in his seat a bit before saying, "You don't have to answer."

Shaking my head, I turned to stare out into the world passing by in a blur. "I don't mind. I've just never spoken a word about my family aloud since I left."

"I guess that makes us similar."

"He was younger than me but only by a year. He'd gone ice skating with a friend. She'd told him she was afraid, and he pressured her into it anyway, without our parents around, which was strictly against their rules. She fell through the lake and couldn't be saved, and he held onto that guilt until it turned him sour. He hardly ate, didn't have any friends, and shut the world out. The goddess came to me and told me I could help save him, and I was so eager to see that light in his eyes, I forgot her warnings."

Atlas placed his hand over mine, stilling it. "I'm sorry, Marley. That must have been awful."

"For everyone involved." I couldn't handle the pressure of the memories nor the look of pity on his face. Combating dealing with my past, I blurted out the question that had been on my mind since the night before. "Where did you go? After your parents kicked you out?"

He cleared his throat, adjusting the reins. "I was twelve, and Bash had just lost his parents. Torryn moved into the castle to help counsel him, and I followed like a lost puppy with nowhere else to go."

"Have you lived there since?"

"That's two questions."

I rolled my eyes. "Fine, you can have two as well."

"Yes. Mostly. I have a place in the village, and I spent some time in the human lands, but the castle has always been home. What about you? Where's home?"

I lifted a shoulder. "Home is wherever I fall asleep, I guess. I don't have one central place. I roam."

His brow darted up. "All the time? Isn't that lonely?"

"That's three questions. You're pushing your luck." I nudged him with my elbow. "Yes, I wander. And no, it's not lonely. At least it wasn't. But now, it feels like it might have been. And, maybe, I hadn't noticed."

That tiny ball of fire kept us toasty warm as winter day melted into winter afternoon. Our questions moved from serious to small things that probably didn't matter to most of the world. But I could tell anyone how fast Atlas could run a mile as a wolf, and he could tell them about my fear of snakes. There was comfort in small details. Still, I watched the tree lines in the distance like a hawk most of the ride. I studied the shadows and the shapes that formed them. I kept an eye behind us, never feeling safe enough to really settle in, but comforted by the company, nonetheless.

Levin had found me so many times. Had beaten me bloody, had tried to drown me. Had tried and failed to curse me. Somehow, I'd escaped, but barely. Every time. As the fear took over, exposed as we were to the elements, I continued our game for distraction. We'd lost track of question debt hours ago.

"I thought Raven lost all of her magic. How is this here?" I jutted my chin toward the ball, keeping my hands tucked in my lap below the bear fur.

"There are loopholes in magic, it seems. And Bastian is very good at loopholes."

"Do other people know?"

"She doesn't hide her power. But until they can be sure this way of doing it cannot be duplicated by others and create another Grimoire situation, they will not be discussing the how's of it all."

Shifting beneath the fur, I shook my head. "I can't imagine being cut off from my power. It would be like losing one of my senses. To not be able to feel the power would be like not being able to see. Or hear."

He looked out the window, suddenly preoccupied as he simply nodded.

"I'm sorry," I whispered. "Losing your ability to shift must have been terrible. Your wolf was so beautiful."

"There's no sense in dwelling on it. Better to just move on."

Reaching for his hand, I squeezed. "No, Atlas. Sometimes it's better to feel what you feel and grieve."

I might as well have been talking to a wall for all the emotional response I got. He blinked three times, and everything haunted on his face, lit solely by the ball of fire, was gone. Replaced with something stoic and methodical. I was beginning to see all the similarities between us to a haunting degree. He clicked his tongue twice, shifting the horses on the path.

Taking advantage of my power, I let a small amount seep forward, if only to convince myself that he was okay. But there was nothing there beyond that black mark. No feelings at all. As if he'd actually cast them away with magic he didn't know he had.

"You're staring," he said finally.

"Sorry, Atlas. Lost in my own thoughts, I guess."

"Call me Atty. Everyone else does. Atlas feels so formal and trite."

"I'll think about it."

He nudged me with his right arm. "Are you hungry?"

"I'm used to traveling quickly and lightly. I'll be okay."

Pulling back on the reins, he called out, "Whoa, fellas." When the sleigh came to a stop, he hopped out and opened a trunk.

"Fish, fruit, bread and cheese. What sounds good?"

"How the hell do you have fruit in winter? I haven't had fruit for months." My stomach growled at the thought.

He flashed a wolfish grin. "I guess it's your lucky day, Frostbite."

Moments later, when he handed me the soft pear, I didn't hesitate as I closed my eyes and sank my teeth into the fleshy side, letting the juice run down my chin, and moaning at the sweet taste. When I pulled the fruit away, I glanced at Atlas to thank him.

Eyes wide and jaw slackened, he audibly swallowed as he reached for another pear and handed it to me without blinking. "Do it again."

I burst into laughter as I swiped the pear. This time taking an obnoxiously large bite and moaning like a wild animal while I wiggled in the seat, batting my eyelashes.

He laughed, grabbing the reins to direct the horses over the stone bridge between the covens. "Ruined it."

8

"Is that Crescent Cottage?"

We had stopped in what used to be the town square in the Moon Coven. Most of the buildings were in utter disrepair, some gone completely. But two women stood together outside of a building I was sure had been destroyed during the Grimoire battle.

"The second version, yes. Come on. They won't bite."

"Was that a shifter joke?" I asked, letting him take my hand.

"No. I'm quite certain Kir would actually bite someone, no matter what her species. Nym's safe though. Stay close to her."

As we neared them, Atlas didn't drop my hand, and I didn't pull away. Both women, one a fierce blonde and the other a stunning brown woman with golden bands on her arms and tied into her hair, kept their eyes locked on our intertwined fingers.

"Blink three times if he's kidnapped you," the blonde woman said in introduction.

"That'll be the biter," Atlas warned. "Ladies, this is Marley. Marley,"—he pointed with his chin—"Kirsi and Nym."

They exchanged a glance before looking me over. Kirsi

seemed far more scrupulous as she scanned me and then the horse-drawn sleigh behind us.

"The red hair tells me you'll kick his ass if he's being a dick. The hand-holding tells me he's trying not to be, but what's the sleigh for?"

"Romance," Nym answered, her smooth voice like honey as she tugged Kirsi closer to her.

"No," we shouted at the same time, dropping our hands. I couldn't help but notice the way Atlas rubbed his palm on his pants before shoving it into his pocket.

"It's just for traveling over the snow," Atty added, shuffling past them.

He whistled low, swinging the door to Crescent Cottage open before stepping inside. I'd been here only once before when I was very young.

"Isn't it incredible?" Nym asked as she gestured for me to follow.

"Rave's going to lose it. I didn't think Bash could outdo last year's Solstice gift, but this one might do it."

"It's exactly the same," Atty said, walking up a narrow aisle and pulling a small glass vial from the shelf. "Every detail."

"He's been taking her there in her dreams so he could get everything just right. And I've been helping, too… obviously," Kirsi said.

"I bought my first elixir from this shelf." I was speaking mostly to myself as I ran a hand over several charmed vials sealed with black wax. "There was an old woman who worked here then. She passed me a sweet when my mother wasn't watching."

"That was Vianna Moonstone, Rave's grandmother. She was everything," Kirsi said.

Atty clapped his hands, breaking the spell over my memory. "So, about this log."

Kirsi and Nym shared a look.

"What?"

"You're not going to like it, but… you're a witch, and she's a witch… You two have to make the salt circle. We can't do it anymore."

"Nope. No magic for me. I'll just go find someone." Atlas moved toward the door. "What was the baker's name?"

"Don't be ridiculous," I said, snatching three white candles from a shelf nearby. "Is it okay if we use these?"

"I'll start you a tab," Kirsi said with a sly smile.

"Great. Her name is Bastian Firepool," Atty said. "Do you need me to spell that for you?"

Nym laughed as she gathered a few bunches of holly and set them on the counter.

Atlas crossed the room and rubbed his fingers along the stone surface, murmuring. "It's so similar, it feels as if Tor could still be lying here."

Kirsi slid a hand into his. "How many times have I told you not to dwell on the past, Pup? Things happen, and we have to move on. Even when they devastate us."

He leaned into her, making her stumble, just to throw his enormous size around. "I wasn't dwelling."

Their close bond filled the room. I'd had nothing like that, and I hadn't seen him so comfortable with someone. She poked him in the ribs for retaliation, and he mussed her hair. As she took a swing at him, I realized, if I hadn't seen his past, they could have passed for siblings.

"I have the best idea." Atlas straightened, his eyes brightening. "You guys should come with us."

Kirsi snorted. "Not on your life."

"Aw. Come on. There's plenty of room."

There certainly wasn't plenty of room. Maybe for one of them, but the four of us crammed into that magically covered sleigh would be cramped. I stared at Atlas, hoping one of his hidden spells was mind reading. But as he nudged Kirsi again, I knew he was wholly unaware of my thoughts. I couldn't decide if he was nervous to be alone with me or simply didn't want me there at all. Probably both. He hadn't signed up for this, but neither had I.

She paused, studying his face for several moments before looking back at me, and then dragged him off to a room in the back, behind a wall of floor-length ivy, creating a faux door.

Their voices were too quiet to hear anything, but as Nym approached with a few more things in her arms, she sighed. "Never mind them. Sometimes they live in their own little world."

"It's really great that he has a close bond with someone."

She paused, sweeping another glance over me. "When did you say you and Atty met?"

"Oh, um. Not too long ago."

Her green eyes narrowed further. "It's just that Atlas doesn't... Women to Atlas are..."

"Believe me, I know."

"You do?"

"Atlas and I are not a couple or anything remotely close. We decided to do this thing for the king together, and..." I lifted a shoulder, turning to stare out the window. "It's not like that."

"Oh, okay. Well then, I guess you don't need the warning."

Surprised, I looked back at her. "Atlas doesn't need a warning. Everybody's got a past."

She shifted the golden bands on her arm as she removed the cork from a bottle, spreading the salt on the floor. "I'm only saying guard your heart. He's prone to breaking them."

The ivy hanging down the wall swayed just as Nym finished creating the salt circle.

"Tell the pup there's not enough coins in the world to convince you to go traipsing around the territories in winter in a fucking horse-drawn sleigh."

Nym tossed Atlas a candle, and he caught it with ease. "I think I'll pass, Atty."

"Come on, guys. Don't make me go by myself."

The words slipped from him with so much ease, had Nym not gasped, he might not have caught the mistake in his words. My presence was nothing. I was nothing. And he obviously wanted to make sure I knew that.

"I mean… You know what I mean," he said, stumbling over himself.

Had he told Kirsi of my power and hoped they could become a wedge? A guarantee that nothing would come of this pull between us? As if I couldn't be trusted. I had my own mind. My own self-control… mostly. Setting my jaw, I gathered the holly and walked to the salt circle, laying the greenery at the northern and southernmost points. I had to follow him around, but I certainly didn't have to take it any further than what this was. A job.

The second I'd left home, I abandoned those who would ever love and support me. That was the choice I'd made, and it had been the right one. I couldn't deny the loneliness seeping over me, though. In the presence of genuine friendship and familial bonds, that giant hole in my heart throbbed. Even if I failed to admit it, I was jealous. I hadn't been enough company for Atlas.

"Do you have a log?" I asked, looking only at Nym, scared to show the isolation roaring through me.

"I left it in the back. Can you grab it, Atty?"

When Atlas disappeared, Kirsi turned, leaning close to whisper. "Whatever is going on between you two is your business. But if you're planning on hurting him, I'll hunt you down. We know the witches don't all accept him as one of their own. He's stuck in the middle of who he was and who he is now. If you're spying for someone to get to the king's council, there's no place you can hide that we will not find you."

"Enough, Kir," Nym stepped in. "She gets it."

Her words were like a knife to a fresh wound. My mind had put me in a vulnerable state, and I wasn't ready for them. Everyone would have preferred it if I weren't here at all. I certainly would have.

"This is a mistake," I said, dusting my hands. "You should let him find someone else." Though the door knob stuck, I managed to escape the confinements of the walls sinking in on me before Atlas returned.

I should have stayed and helped with the spell I knew he would struggle with, but he didn't want me there and neither did his friends. Story of my entire life. No one wanted me around.

Sitting beneath that magical ball of fire, I stared anywhere but at the door. I couldn't get far enough away from them, and yet I had to stay close in order to protect him. The balance was nauseating. Nym's warning mixed with Kirsi's threat had changed nothing, really. But it put me in a place to evaluate my situation, and I didn't want to do that either.

Even though Atlas was broken, perhaps a piece of my soul was marked as well. The soft sound of the door clicking shut startled me. I turned, half expecting that lopsided grin. Instead, Kirsi stood there, arms over her chest, gray eyes staring me down.

"He can't do it on his own, and we can't help him."

Standing, I let the fur slide from my lap as I exited the sleigh and walked to the door, meeting her toe-to-toe as I hid the pit of my despair, turning into something stronger than I really was. "I can appreciate you worrying about your friend, but I won't tolerate threats. I don't know what he said to you, but I'm not a bad person. You want to threaten me? You're going to have to hear what I have to say back. Otherwise, I'll just leave."

Her eyes narrowed. "I'm listening."

"I've lived through moments with him that you will never experience. You don't know my heart or my intentions. You don't even fucking know me, shifter. And that's fine. Except one day, he will find someone real, someone that he can open up to and love. And if you speak to her like you just spoke to me, if she is weak of heart in any way, she's going to run. Far and fast and it will be all your fault. So, watch what you say. Or you will be the reason that man is alone forever."

The glare melted into a conspiratorial smile. "The fire suits you. But never call me a shifter again."

She held the door open for me as I entered, staring into the stern faces of Atlas and Nym.

"Relax," Kirsi said, hanging an arm over my shoulder. "We're best friends now."

I didn't give away an ounce of what I was feeling. Instead, I slipped off my boots and stepped to the edge of the circle, only looking at Atlas long enough to acknowledge he should do the same.

"It's not a spell like the ones from receivings. You have to ground yourself by imagining thick roots growing from your feet and winding around the middle of the Earth, anchoring you."

Following Nym's instructions, Atlas closed his eyes, a bead of sweat dripping down his temple, though the inside of Crescent Cottage remained chilly. I did not have to cast to sense the apprehension rolling off of him as he set the Yule log in the center of the salt circle.

The two shifters stepped away. Atlas wouldn't know what to do for this blessing, but I did. I only hoped the goddess didn't show up as I spoke the traditional incantation.

"Moon above, earth below, Goddess, we call unto thee. As the candles burn, so the year turns, bring us health, luck, and prosperity. Intentions set, power met, blessings be."

The force radiating from Atlas mixed with my own and sat below my skin. That string between us seemed to tighten, and I wondered if he felt it, too. Far too soon, or maybe not soon enough, the magic from the spell melted around us like warm honey, coating the Moon Coven Yule log. One down, five to go. Though perhaps I would not be here for all of them. I only needed to get through Future's visit.

"Did Bash leave you a door?" Atlas asked moments later as we walked out.

"No," Nym answered. "Kirsi and I have a bet. She thinks she can beat me back. But Talon was always faster than Scoop."

"I could have beaten both of you," Atlas said, masking the sadness well enough for the others to miss it, though I did not. "My money's on Nym. Kirsi stops for naps."

"I'll kick your ass, Atty."

"Not on your best day and my worst, Ghosty."

Kirsi shared a wink before shifting into a giant black panther and tearing off down the road. With a roar, Nym followed, the heavy paws of a white tiger pounding the ground as she caught her lover.

Atlas opened his mouth to speak, but I stopped him. "I know you don't want to be alone with me. I respect and understand that, if not for this unique situation, you wouldn't have to deal with me. However, I'm still a person, and I have feelings. I know why you wanted them to come, but you don't have to worry about me. I won't be touching you again."

"Marley—"

"I'm serious, Atlas. I can't be the person who puts the broken man back together. Or the unwanted one all the time. That's the Spirits' task. I'm here to see this job through, and then be on my way. No touching. No attachments. You don't need to be uncomfortable around me. Consider it self-preservation for both of us."

I was in the sleigh, smashing myself all the way over before he stepped away from the spot where he stood, stunned. It wasn't a punch in the face, like Laramie's introduction, but hopefully I'd made my point clear.

He didn't say a word. The sleigh jostled when he grabbed the handle and helped himself inside, but he didn't move the blankets or furs over his lap. Didn't even bother to glance in my direction. Simply reached for the reins, snapped them once, and sat as still as a statue as we lurched forward.

After an hour of traveling through the Moon Coven, much of it barren trees and scattered homes, he pulled the sleigh to a stop. At first, I'd wondered if he could feel my nerves building the further east we traveled. But when I cast out of habit mostly, there was no awareness there. Simply anger. The silence between us could not have been louder. Still, there wasn't an ounce of me that wanted to apologize.

"We'll sleep here for the night."

"In the middle of the woods? This isn't... safe."

"Afraid your Spirits won't be able to navigate the trees?" Spoken another time, it would have borne a playful tone. His signature. But this was different. *He* was different. Whatever fragile thing that might have bloomed between us had broken when I walked away.

I ground my teeth. "My enemies are not of the spiritual world. They are very much of this one. And if you thought outside yourself for one moment, you wouldn't degrade me for an emotion as relevant as fear."

"I think the only thing that can break the dome is my power. It's a magical shield. We are perfectly safe," he said, staring straight ahead. "But some space would be good for both of us."

Encasing Raven's flame in a glass orb, he snatched it from the sleigh and stepped out, yanking all but one blanket with him. "Come on."

The second that ball of warmth was gone, the chill set in. I reluctantly followed him out of the covered sleigh, sinking into the deep snow. Three giant Atlas strides later, he cast a slightly larger glass dome and released the orb, setting it to float above us. He silently tossed the furs over the snow and topped them with the blankets.

When he left to check on the horses, I cast, enlarging the tiny pillows from my pocket. Atlas opened a box and pulled out a sack of food for the beasts, stopping to drop off dried meat, a few slices of cheese, and another pear before tending to the animals.

I waited for him. I'd been harsh. Mean even. Because that's the only way I knew how to protect myself when I couldn't run away.

He did not come back. He leaped into the sleigh, wrapped the last blanket around his legs, and looked up at the bright moon in the sky. I wondered if he could feel me staring at him. He could not sleep in that cold. And the closer we got to midnight, the more of a chance there was of being visited by a Spirit again.

I turned away until his dome fogged over. He shivered, trying and failing to stretch the blanket over his long legs. I cast toward him, wondering what he was feeling, and the misery was overwhelming. As if he'd taken a dark turn and let it swallow him. Unable to bear it, I lay down, turning my back to him again.

He'd sealed me into the dome, and I couldn't get out if I wanted to. But when I closed my eyes, I could only see a stubborn Atlas, shivering, lips blue and cheeks flushed. Goddess be damned. I wasn't supposed to care. He was a mark. Just a job to finish and move on. It didn't matter, though. I already cared, and I was fooling myself for thinking otherwise.

I stood, banging on the glass, certain he could hear me and ignored it. I even screamed at him, letting my voice alert all things nearby where we were and that someone might have been in trouble. Nothing worked. I was going to have to use magic. He'd hate me more for it if his reaction to the spell circle today was any indication. This would not be the power of True Sight. No. I would have to do something far more annoying.

I cast toward the sleigh without giving myself too much time to think about it. And when he squirmed, I held my breath, wondering if I'd be prepared enough for the backlash of an angry Atlas.

9

It wasn't a spell that would win me any battles. Not even one that could protect me. And truly, as the man stood, his shirt slowly unraveling thread by thread, I wondered what the hell I was thinking when he was already so cold. Atlas yelped and slammed the door open, redder than an autumn apple.

"What the fuck is this?" he yelled.

I darted outside, not realizing how scary being locked in had been, until I was free. "You cannot sleep in the sleigh. It's too cold."

"Your solution is to take away the few bits of covering I have?" he shouted, his shirt now only a long string trailing behind him as he stomped toward me. "Get back in your dome."

"I'm not getting in there until you do."

Grabbing the ends of his hair, he looked at the sky and growled. Very much the wolf.

"How the fuck are you the most infuriating woman on the planet the second we're stuck together?"

Jamming my hands on my hips, ignoring the numbing of my

toes, I answered. "I saw how well that worked for you, and I decided to copy."

Atlas' jaw ticked as he closed the space between us, grabbing the ends of my hair as he forced me to look up at him. He was furious. Heaving breaths and hard eyes. But the second he looked into my gaze, something calmed. "This red hair is going to be the end of me."

"Not if you freeze to death first," I whispered, suddenly aware that I'd forgotten to stop the spell and the man was almost naked, towering over me. "We can share the heat, you stubborn, foolish man."

I couldn't see the mind racing behind the eyes that gave nothing else away, but I could feel all of his emotions tumbling like a ship lost in a raging sea.

I placed my palms onto his bare chest. "I know you're mad, and I'm difficult, and this situation isn't ideal for either of us, but if we don't accept it for what it is, we're going to be miserable. I'm sorry I got so upset."

"I'm sorry for making you feel like you were unwanted. I know what that feels like, and I'm ashamed of myself. I won't make excuses." He swallowed. "There's something here, and I don't know how I feel about it. Or how I'm supposed to feel about it. I don't know if it's genuine or just this damn magic. It takes the truth out of everything."

"I thought I was the only one that could feel it. Maybe you're right, and that's all it is."

His gaze shifted between mine, his giant, frozen fingers brushing my cheeks. "Can I have my clothes back now? Or do you have more devious plans for me, Frostbite?"

I jumped away from him, casting to repair the clothing as we moved into the warmth. Any coherent thought I might have had vanished, settling within the deep grooves of his muscled chest. The ache to touch him became overwhelming as that shirt reformed, so, so slowly.

"Don't look at me like that."

My breath caught in my throat. "I wasn't… I didn't… Be less fucking attractive then."

His lopsided grin reappeared. "Where's the fun in that?"

Lifting a blanket from the ground, I rolled my eyes. "Just stay on your side, Wolf."

"Again, I say, where's the fun in that?"

"You don't want to be half-naked and on top of me if the Spirits show up."

He tilted his head to the side, scanning me once before answering. "I'm pretty sure I do."

"No," I laughed, holding out a hand. "You take that side, and I'll take this one. We sleep apart. No touching."

"No touching. Got it."

When we'd settled in, a pillow between us, his breathing slowed, and I thought maybe he'd already fallen asleep until he whispered, "You never accepted my apology." I turned to face him, and he slid the pillow down, so he could look at me. "Will you forgive me?"

"I guess. And I'm half sorry I took most of your clothes off."

He chuckled, looking back at the massive moon we lay beneath. "I'm going to disappoint you by the end of this. Maybe I should apologize for that now, too."

"You could choose not to," I whispered, nearly holding my breath.

His pillow crinkled as he shook his head. "The way I feel is not a choice. No matter what your Goddess or anyone else says. And I don't reject women. I'm not afraid of anything. Least of all that. I just like my life the way it is."

I couldn't respond. I'd hoped that something might have been cracking within him. But I wouldn't have been there if it were that easy. So, I rolled away, letting the exhaustion take me.

His whisper pulled me from the cusp of sleep. "Do you think they'll come again tonight?"

I yawned. "I hope not."

He reached over and took my hand, squeezing. "Me, too."

THE SEASON SEEMED TO CHANGE OVERNIGHT, THOUGH I REFUSED to open my eyes. The Spirits didn't come, but I was certain we were being cooked alive within our bubble. Until I twisted and realized it was not, in fact, the change of a season, but a massive man wrapped around me, his hot, slow breaths warming my neck.

It was wrong to want to stay there, and I knew it. Of all the men in the world, this one, specifically, would lead to certain heartache. I needed to harden my feelings and keep him at a distance, but that was a difficult admission. Especially when I remembered what he'd looked like half-naked last night. Freezing cold and steaming mad. Staring at me like he either wanted to end me or ruin me in all the best ways.

The mental image of laying here with him now stirred something within me. I swore I had self-control, but the pillow between us had long gone, and something else rested in its place, pushing firmly against my ass. Even as I tried to talk myself into restraint, I wiggled backward. Not to stir the beast, but only to feel him. To satisfy a craving wrapped in curiosity.

His arm tightened around me, those slow breaths rapidly increasing as he stirred awake, though he did not move away. Feeling his heartbeat against my back, I could tell the second his thoughts changed to mirror mine. I stayed perfectly still, barely chancing a breath as his hand moved from my shoulder, lower and lower, until that massive palm rested at the top of my waistband. He waited, wordless, breathless, for me to urge him forward or make him back off. Together, we danced on the edge of a steep cliff. Though there were no words, I knew this game.

I had no coherent thoughts as I anticipated him going further. Sliding those fingers over me. Into me. He inched closer, dipping below the waistband. My eyes fell shut. Eagerness filled me until I could have melted into a puddle as he moved the tiniest bit.

"You have to say you want it, Frostbite," he rumbled into my ear, the early morning turning his voice into something feral.

I opened my mouth to speak, but I couldn't. Goddess, did I want it. Want him. The pulse between my legs was practically screaming for him to move three inches lower and feel how badly I wanted him. Needed him.

He pressed his lips to the back of my ear and growled, sending a wave of heat down my spine. I had seconds to decide. But my brain and body were at war with each other. And that's how I knew I couldn't follow through. If both parts of me were not willing, then I needed to say no. But damn, did I hate myself for it.

I twisted, turning to face him. Staring into those tired, icy blue eyes. He did not fault me for one second.

Instead, he leaned forward, kissed me on the nose, and said, "Good morning, asshole."

I couldn't help the laughter. I couldn't even help the way that beautiful, lopsided grin felt like the best thing in the world to wake up to. And that was the problem. In days, this would all be over. And while Atlas' heart wasn't ready for me, I thought mine was ready for him. That was a dangerous trail of thoughts that would only lead to heartache.

He stood, blocking himself with the pillow as he adjusted, then immediately folded the blankets as if nothing happened. He waved a hand, and the door appeared in the dome.

"I've got to, uh… take care of some stuff. Give me ten minutes?"

I smirked. "What kind of stuff?"

His grin widened. "Well, Marley... you see when a man wakes up—"

"No. Stop." I buried my head under my pillow. "Just go. I'll be here when you're done playing with yourself."

"It's more fun when two people play," he said, leaving me to my second bout of laughter.

The road to my childhood home was fairly smooth. It came with its own set of reservations, though. And as we crossed back into the Fire Coven, keeping south until we neared the Storm Coven border, the conversation between Atlas and I became non-existent. With the clouds gathering in the distance, the promise of a blizzard on the horizon, I felt that familiar pressing fear. Levin Riverden knew where I once lived. He'd made it his business to know everything there was to possibly know.

I watched the tree line, holding my breath with every sign of movement. I tried not to look back, fearful of alarming Atlas. But by late morning, he pulled the reins to the side and stopped the horses. He stared straight ahead for several seconds before facing me, the scar on his face skewing as he lifted his eyebrow in question.

"What?" I asked.

"When I met you, you watched the door as often as everything else. When you let me in your room after Past visited, you kept an eye on the hall. Last night, you said you had enemies in this world. Tell me what you are afraid of."

I picked at my fingernails, unable to look up. "It's not a 'what'. It's a 'who.'"

Reaching over, he tucked a finger under my chin, forcing my eyes to his. "I would never let something happen to you on this job. You know that, right?"

"Yesterday, you locked me in a bubble and tried to freeze yourself to death. I don't think your decisions can be relied upon from one moment to the next." I kept a light, playful tone, but he was having none of it.

"Marley. I mean it. You can question everything else about me, but that is one thing I will not falter on. You are safe, but you have to tell me who we're looking for."

"His name is Levin Riverden. He's a swamp witch."

"Tell me why you fear him."

"He's almost killed me twice. He nearly drowned me last year."

"He was one of your marks?"

I nodded, turning to look out the window. "He didn't make the right choice. He'd killed someone when he was younger, and the goddess thought he was still redeemable. He spent so much of his life pushing people away, afraid of what his magic could do. And when I approached him, I really thought he could be saved, too."

"He couldn't?"

"Sometimes, your heart makes the choice for you, and it doesn't matter what you say to Future. Levin's damned. He has no one. And he's convinced himself that if he kills me, the curse over him will be broken."

Atlas sat back, gathering the reins in his hands once more. "Sometimes, our brains and our hearts are at war with one another, and no matter how much we wish things could be different, the cards didn't play in our favor, Marley. If he comes near you, I'll kill him. But I understand why he failed to change."

True Sight told me Atlas had become far more nervous as the sleigh powered forward. Maybe he thought he could talk his way out of Future's damnation. His mind seemed to race beside me as he became more vigilant. Watching for movement as much as I was.

"What do you know of his spells?" he finally asked.

"He can control water. He has incredible strength and—"

In a flash, Atlas went rigid, his eyes glossing over as they glowed from within.

A receiving.

10

The timing could not have been worse. One moment, he was promising he would protect me, and the next, he was trapped in the realm where witches traveled to acquire new spells. We'd have to sit here, completely helpless, until his soul returned to his body. But he would have new magic, and maybe that was something he needed. Strength in power meant strength of the man. Someday, I hoped he'd learn to stop fearing it.

As I sat, waiting for him to return, I wondered if the horses were cold. I considered hopping out to feed them a snack, since we hadn't let them rest much today, but the second I contemplated leaving the protection of the dome, if I even could, I shied away and sat back down, my fear debilitating.

When the goddess had met me in the receiving realm to introduce me to her Spirits and *bless* me with the gift of calling them, damning and rescuing witches for the rest of my life, I'd cried inside. I'd wanted something to protect myself so badly, and, instead, I got *them*. Three Spirits with poor attitudes, questionable humor, and a penchant for judgment.

Minutes seemed to turn into an hour as Atlas remained within the magical realm, and I worried as the storm clouds ahead moved over us, and the snow fell.

"I fucking hate that," he said at last. "Leaving myself to be murdered by any random passerby because I have no way to defend myself while I get dropped in the middle of a giant puzzle until I can figure it out."

I forced a smile, unwilling to show my instant relief. "The marking is beautiful, though."

He looked down to his arm to see three diagonal lines with a half moon over the top of them and two tiny diamonds below. Without a word, Atlas pulled his sleeve down and took the reins.

"It looks like today's storm will be that blizzard," I said, to change the conversation.

"Yeah. We'd better feed the horses."

"And ourselves," I added when his stomach growled.

There was no sense in being afraid of a storm in this coven, so after our meal, we took off. If it wasn't a blizzard, it could be treacherous lightning or tropical storms, and that would have been far more dangerous for us all.

Though it became difficult to see, we made it to a nearby tunnel entrance with an overhang for the horses to rest. The gray sunlight faded away once we left them and the carriage tied up and began our trek through the hollowed, underground tunnel, lit with scattered torches. In many ways, my childhood hovered around us. In the smell of metal lingering in the air, the echo of faraway voices guiding us onward, even the dim lighting. But by the time we'd left the sleigh behind, I was nearly crawling out of my skin with anxiety. My stomach churned, and my bones rattled.

Atlas wrapped an arm over my shoulder, slowing us. "Trust me, Frostbite. I won't leave you."

Yet.

The unspoken word drifted between us..

"Do you want to stop anywhere and see your parents or friends or anything?"

"No," I breathed. "Let's just make this quick."

"Are you sure? Because I really don't mind."

Slowing my pace, I stepped away from him. "I left my parents long ago and since I've never had a marked Storm Coven witch, I haven't returned. And I'm grateful for it. I don't want to linger."

"But if you did..."

"I don't."

We'd have to go to the River Coven next, and I needed as much time back in that sleigh to prepare as possible. I'd spent a lot of these last years in fear of dying, and whatever backbone I'd once possessed had left me for humble caution. I no longer had it in me to face unbearable heartache, and that included looking into the face of my parents, knowing I was responsible for the death of the child that had been the perfect blend of both of them.

As if he could read my thoughts, Atty took my hand. "If I have to deal with my past, maybe you should, too."

"I'm not really a fan of practicing what I preach."

He shared a sad smile. "I wasn't really a fan of watching my father kick me out or seeing Laramie die all over again."

"How does a promise to come meet them another time sound?"

I had him there, and he knew it. He'd have to commit to something with me, and that was his weakness. But I wasn't ready. Hypocrite or not, I could not look them in the face.

"Fine. I won't push it."

He saw my conviction and accepted it, turning on a heel to keep going. "Did you live in these tunnels as a child, or are there houses down here?"

"There are certain paths that cut off in many directions toward separate pods. The pods are the homes."

"I guess the Storm Coven witches have no issues with claustrophobia," he said, clearing his throat.

"If the walls feel like they're moving in on you, watch your feet and keep steady breaths."

He nudged me. "I never said I was afraid."

"Neither did I." I winked.

"Where are we going here, anyway?"

I lifted a shoulder, happy to let the conversation go in a different direction. "I have no idea. The king sent you, not me."

"You are so helpful. Has anyone ever told you that before?"

"Daily." I tugged him forward. "Come on. There'll be a pod at the end of the tunnel. We can ask someone there, I'm sure."

The underground hallway narrowed as we moved further down and through. His broad shoulders seemed to graze the walls as we walked, and I wondered if he'd complain, but instead, he whistled a tune, smiling when the sound echoed. We carried on like that until he jerked to a stop.

"Did you hear that?"

"It's just the pod."

"I've only been to the outskirts to meet with a group of silenced witches. I'd heard of this, but to see it is bizarre."

"If you lived where the land tried to kill you on a daily basis, you'd hide too."

"Fair point well made."

The pod ahead buzzed with excited voices that grew as we drew near. Two witches stood at the entrance, one with a smile and the other more rigid.

"We're here to gather the Yule log for the Solstice celebration," Atlas said, his voice more formal and deep than his casual tone.

"Yes. They warned us you'd be coming," the rigid man said, resting his hand on the door as if he wouldn't let us in.

Warned by whom, I wasn't sure.

But Atlas did not take the bait. Instead, he slid his hands into his pockets and grew three inches until he stared down at the man. "Good, then you'll be quick about it."

The man's eyes bulged in reaction to the fierce tone. My heart skipped a beat, but for a completely different reason, as that voice reminded me of the growl in my ear this morning.

"Don't bother with him," the other witch said, pushing her brown hair over her shoulder. "He missed breakfast. I'll go get the log for you. They've already done the blessing."

I could sense Atlas' relief. He would not want to perform magic in front of a coven, especially as a representative of the king during this fragile time. The woman didn't enter the room behind her. She turned down the adjacent hall, moving in a light jog. While we waited, Atlas spent his time trying and succeeding at intimidating the guard with a stare down.

When the witch returned, she wished us a Happy Solstice, and we were on our way to the dreaded River Coven within the hour. I hadn't been back since Levin. I would have been forced to return if another witch from this territory had been marked, but somehow, I was spared the mental torture. Still, as the sun dropped, the ground around us turning to icy ponds rather than pillowy snow, I couldn't help the way my hands shook with fear.

Atlas reached over, pulling me toward him, and fuck if I didn't let him. He was security when I needed it most. A companion I'd never really realized I was missing until now.

"If you see anything alarming, shout. He's only one man."

And he was, truly, but my brain told me otherwise. Nearing the swamps, carefully leading the sled along the banks, I counted the minutes until I could take another breath.

"We have to go over this ridge, and there should be another group that knows we're coming. I've been here before. We'll get the log and leave as fast as possible."

"Okay," I whispered. "I trust you."

11

Atlas leaned over and patted the top of my hand before tugging the reins back. Over the ridge and down a hill, a small village of cottages sat nestled together. The warm glow of the lanterns hanging outside their homes created an ambiance that would have looked safe to anyone none the wiser. Billowing puffs of smoke rose from chimneys, leaving the comforting scent of winter, of freshly burned wood and sawdust, in the air.

"Do you want to stay locked in the dome?" Atlas asked, his hand resting on the magical door.

"You couldn't pay me enough money to sit out here by myself. I don't even want to leave the horses."

"Those four are Bastian's personal stallions. They are fearless and smart. Should a threat come, they'll be safer than both of us. Just remember the River Coven hasn't taken the merge of the covens very well. They won't be fans of ours."

"Why can't we cut down a tree and get the hell out of here?" I grumbled, knowing the answer before I asked it.

"The territory must give it freely. That's how it works, I guess."

"Yeah, yeah. I know. Let's get this over with."

The witch that answered the first cottage door slammed it in our faces. Unfazed, as with most things, Atlas simply trudged on to the next. By the third rejection, although he held that smile, his knuckles had gone white by his side, and I could tell his patience was wearing thin.

"Next year, I'm dragging Bash's ass through this shit."

The fourth and fifth doors never opened. Though we knocked, could hear the people inside, and see the lamps glowing, they didn't bother with us. The rejection was taking the edge off the paranoia, but as we approached the last home, a strange sense of panic set in.

"Wait," I said, grabbing Atlas' fist before it could connect with the door. "This is the last house. We need to catch them."

He sighed. "I'm trying, Frostbite."

"Just give me a second. I have a True Sight spell. Maybe I can find them."

I cast, letting magic guide me. It was really only to know people's feelings, but if they were further away, the magic took longer to work, almost as if a link formed between me and the person. I'd never used the power to find someone, but if there was an emotion, I could feel it.

"Someone is moving away from us. I think they're in the back."

He was gone in a flash, and I could barely keep up as we rounded the corner, and a boy came into sight, his back to us as he scurried into the mass of dead trees behind the home. As we neared and Atlas shouted for him to stop, the boy froze.

He turned slowly, his sour face holding a scowl. "If you come any closer, I'll cast fire and burn it here and now."

"Why?" The word was out of my mouth before I could even think it through.

"The king is no real king. Ask my father. He says he's a dick tato."

"A dictator?" Atlas asked with a smile, taking a small step forward.

The boy moved backward, the log snug in his arms.

He lifted his hands to the boy, palms out. "We're not here to cause trouble, little guy. Just give us the log, and we'll be on our way."

The boy propped the log a little higher in his grip so he could free a hand. He looked Atty square in the face as a flame burst to life in his palm. Behind us, a door slammed open and before we could react at all, a woman's voice screeched through the frozen air. "Charles Rivergrain, you put that log down right this instant."

A plump, little woman stood with fists on her hips as she glared at the boy, face red with fury.

"Didn't detect that one?" Atlas whispered.

"I didn't even know if it would work when I picked up on the kid," I hissed back.

"But, Ma... You heard Father last night. This holiday shouldn't be about the dick tato's demands. He should do something for us instead."

The woman stormed forward just as he extinguished his flame. She grabbed Charles by the ear and dragged him to stand before Atlas, who somehow seemed to grow ten feet as he stared down at the boy. There could have been malice in his eyes, hatred for the way he spoke about Bash. But instead, he took a knee. Though still taller than the boy, he made himself small.

"May I please have your Yule log?"

Charles rolled his eyes and plopped the log into Atlas' arms.

"I know what it's like to hear the preachings of your elders and feel that burn to follow. It's so much easier to hate someone than it is to understand them. But as a representative of King Bastian Firepool, he's asked me to deliver something to you.

Because he would never want to take something from you without also giving back."

The hardness in the boy's eyes faltered for just a flash.

"I could keep it," Atlas said. "If you don't want it. Even though he sent it especially for you."

"You're lying."

Atty stood, shrugging. "Suit yourself. Come on, Marley, we've gotta get out of here."

Reaching for my hand, he walked away.

Charles' shout interrupted the woman's quiet lecturing. "Wait."

"Oh sorry, did you say something?" Atlas asked with a grin.

"Far as I can tell, the king owes me anyway. After all, I had to help my mother with the stinking spell."

We got no further than three steps beyond the front of the cottage when faces appeared in the windows. The boy, for all his sass, shied away from the stares, moving closer to his mother's skirts.

She hugged him to her side. "Charles, my darling, one day you will learn that kindness breeds kindness, no matter the past. Your father should not encourage you so."

"But the Dark King…"

"Had his magic taken away trying to rid this world of the real evil," I finished. "I have to believe if someone can make that kind of sacrifice and still fight for our power, they must have some good in them."

Atlas squeezed my hand. "Marley's from Storm. She's not so sure about our king yet, either."

"But I want to be. I want more for this world than a neighbor that will not open a door out of spite. Solstice is a time of rebirth and joy. We should embrace that and try to be better, even when it's hard."

The boy didn't say another word until his brown eyes landed on the sleigh and the massive black beasts pulling it.

"Whoa," he whispered, stepping quietly to the horses, as if he might spook them.

Atlas winked before circling to the back of the sleigh, taking several minutes while the boy and his mother ran their fingers down the shiny manes of the giant horses who nickered and kicked with impatience, ready to leave as much as we were.

When Atlas returned, beaming, he held a piece of paper rolled up and tied with a string that looked an awful lot like the one that had been tying the grain sacks together. I didn't have to wait long to figure out what he was up to.

Charles eagerly pulled the string from the rolled parchment and studied it for several seconds before handing it to his mother. "I can't read the big words yet."

"I struggle with those myself," Atty said, absolutely lying through his teeth.

"This is... you cannot... Is this real?" the mother asked.

"That's King Bastian's signature on the bottom, isn't it?"

In confusion, I sent a questionable glance at Atlas.

The woman grabbed the little boy's hand, thanked us profusely, and dragged her son back down the road in a hurry, as if she had to tell the world a secret I wasn't privy to.

I rounded on Atlas, narrowing my eyes. "What did you do?"

"Let's just say Bash is going to kill me when he finds out I gave away one of his horses, and it's being picked at the Solstice celebration."

I gasped. "You're not serious."

He lifted me into the sleigh and followed, squeezing his eyes shut with a heavy breath to cast his magical door before sitting. "There was a lesson to be learned there. They had a broken wagon behind their house, and you saw how he looked at the team. The horse will help that family more than any guidance I could have offered. And now, it's a guarantee they will come to the celebration and experience something most here never have."

I melted, leaning my head onto his shoulder. "I promise I won't tell anyone that you're actually a really nice person."

"Probably for the best."

Maybe we hadn't changed the world or even most of the minds. But that one little boy, with all his conviction, may one day stand for the king, and that had to mean something. The River Coven was the scariest place I could be, but those moments made it worth it.

The journey became treacherous. We seemed to inch along, guiding the horses carefully through the thick frozen marsh as we tried to make our way back to the bridge leading to the Fire Coven, to carry us further northeast toward Forest.

"Was this here before?" Atlas pulled the sleigh to a complete stop at the edge of a giant, frozen pond intersecting the small bit of path we'd found.

"I think if we had to cross this before, we would have remembered." I scooted forward, looking beyond the beasts to the icy terrain.

"We must have turned the wrong way." Atlas looked over his shoulder. "This whole territory looks the fucking same."

"Can we go around?"

"We're too wide. The marsh on both sides is soft. We're going to have to cross."

"Okay," I said, nodding my head with a deep breath. "Slow and steady."

"You psyching yourself up right now, Frostbite?"

"Absolutely. We should test the ice and see how thick it is first, right?"

"I've got a hatchet. Hold the reins tight, and don't let them follow me."

Fingers shaking, I did as he said, watching as he hopped out of our warm sleigh and into the freezing tundra of the River Coven, digging a hatchet out of a saddlebag before trudging through the deep snow to the edge of the lake.

One swing, two, and three before he managed a breath, the plumes wafting around him as he jerked upright, staring at the horizon. He looked back at me, gestured something with his hands and waited.

I couldn't... didn't understand.

Again, he waved a hand and pointed to his heart, then eyes.

I leaned out of the carriage, careful to keep the reins tight. "What?"

"Dammit, woman. Magic." He flailed his arms. "True Sight." He pointed to his heart and eyes dramatically. "Can you tell if anyone is out there?"

Fear rocked me backward. He wouldn't have asked if he hadn't suspected something. I cast immediately, seeking any kind of emotion beyond the horses and the beautiful man standing on the ice with only a hatchet. Silence. Pure, blissful silence met my power. Thank the goddess.

I shook my head, and he got back to work. Maybe it was precautionary. Still, as he chipped away at the lake, I swept that power back and forth in front of us, seeking anything that might come within range. Eventually, Atlas knelt to the ground and stuck his arm into the hole he'd made.

When he returned, the crinkle of worry in his eyes was enough to overpower the feeling of conviction surrounding him. I instantly felt the same, accepting his emotions as my own.

"I won't sugarcoat it." He pulled the hat from his head. "It's deep ice, but I don't know if it's enough. The sleigh is heavy, and four horses are more so. We can try taking two across. You can stay there, and I'll go back for the other two and the sleigh to make it as safe as possible."

"If you think that's best," I said, keeping the worry from my voice as I stood.

He unhitched the beasts quickly, using his magic to seal Queen Raven's ball of fire in a sphere again so I would have it while I waited for him to come back across.

"We'll walk instead of riding them to distribute our weight across the ice. If you hear anything, the smallest crack, lift your hand like this, but don't shout and startle the horses."

"Okay."

He dropped the reins to the nearest animal and came to stand before me, gripping the sides of my face with gloved hands. "It'll be over before you know it. But if you're scared, I'll go first by myself."

"You're sure we can't go around it?"

His eyes didn't leave mine as he shook his head. "The marsh is too dangerous. We'll be stuck in mud."

"What if I shrink the sleigh?" I couldn't blame him for not considering magic when he'd been so averse to it, but I should have thought of it sooner.

"Can you shrink the horses?"

"No. Nothing with a heartbeat. Only physical items."

"Then we take two horses and you put the sleigh in your pocket. I'll come back for the other two."

I nodded with a swallow. "Okay."

The first step onto the ice was the scariest. He held my hand, refusing to let go, even when his horse hesitated. Inch by inch, it seemed, we moved across the slippery surface.

He spoke words meant to calm the horses, though they did something for me, too. "One time, when I was a boy, just a little older than Charles, I bet Torryn that I could swim across a lake faster than he could. I was young and dumb and getting into that cocky preteen stage.

"When we got to the halfway point, I realized I'd gone as far as I could. Hadn't paced myself, and, as each of my muscles cramped up, I fell behind. The bottom of the lake became a magnet, pulling me down. He saved me, of course. He was always going to win that race. But his words stuck with me, even to this day. Should the water sweep you under, never lose the fight."

He was quiet for a moment, and the horses reacted, pulling backward.

"Keep going," I whispered, my foot slipping as I tried to steady the beast.

When I was stable, he continued. "I'm always fighting. Myself mostly. I know I should let go of all those things Past showed us, and trust me, there's a lot more. But something in me fights to hold on to it. It's as if I am afraid that letting go of the fear will take away the memories. I want to be afraid. I never want to forget the way it made me feel to lie there and watch her die. Even when it hurts to remember."

I was so distracted by his confession, so moved, I didn't hear the first crack. But the second was deafening.

12

"Let go of the horse, Marley," Atlas demanded. "No sudden movements."

"We'll lose them," I protested, heart racing a million miles a minute as my grip tightened so hard around the leather straps, my knuckles lost all color.

"Let go of the fucking horse."

But it didn't matter what he said. Not as a shout came across the lake that took every ounce of self-preservation and strangled it. "Marley Stormborn."

The hair lifted on my arms and down my spine, and my bladder threatened to empty.

"Run," I screamed, dropping the reins and spinning. "It's him. Run, Atty."

But the second I said his name, the lake shattered into hundreds of giant pieces of ice, riding the top of an angry body of water. When the chunk below us tilted, the horses panicked. I panicked.

Atlas pulled the hatchet from his belt and slammed it into the ice below.

"Magic, Atty. We can float in an orb."

He cast, saving the horses near the edge of the slab first. I lost my footing and dropped, slamming my head onto the ice as it continued to rock. Sliding past Atlas, he reached a hand out, rescuing me from the cold water not a second too soon. Another glacier collided with the underbelly of ours, threatening to tip us completely over as he now hung from the hatchet, and I clung to him.

"I have to let go in order to cast again," he shouted. "Trust me."

I nodded frantically, looking over my shoulder to see a man with pitch black hair and deep-set eyes walking across the top of the water as if it were a paved road.

In one motion, Atlas released the hatchet and cast, catching us in a bubble less than a second before we slammed into the dangerous water.

"I'm sorry I forgot to keep checking the banks," I said, hustling to my feet.

"There's no time for that now. Remind me of his spells? Quickly."

"Uhm. Water. And temperature. And..." I could hardly think straight. "He's fast. And stronger than he should be."

"So am I," Atty growled. "Walk backward."

We traveled along the top of the water for mere feet before Levin conjured a geyser below us, and we crashed into each other while the orb spun out of control. Atlas and I scrambled, tumbling until I'd taken an elbow to the face and him a knee to the gut. He reached forward, grabbing and holding me tightly to him so we were one.

We struggled but somehow got to our feet, running the same way the sphere turned. Out of desperation, I called the Spirits. I didn't have self-defense magic. I didn't even have elemental magic. It was a move made in despair, but no one answered.

Atlas roared, slamming his hand into the orb as he stared at the man responsible, who hadn't said more than my name, only conducted chaos.

"I'm going to do something really fucking stupid," Atty said. "You're going to have to trust me. And don't fucking die."

Before I could respond, the bubble around us burst, and I was falling. So was he. Seconds before I crashed into the icy water, he caught me in magic again. Another sphere and a blast of powerful wind slammed into me, throwing me more than halfway across the lake. But he hadn't saved himself.

I screamed in horror as he crashed into the ice-filled water with glaciers so large they could have crushed him or trapped him below. He swam as if the temperature hadn't shocked his body, though I knew that to be impossible. Levin wasn't worried about Atty, though, only me. He flexed his arms forward and cast, but Atlas came from nowhere, tackling Levin to the ground.

In a single move of self-preservation, Levin refroze the entire lake, likely afraid to drown… The irony. I was only a bystander now, trapped in the glass orb to watch as the men, with more strength and speed than either of them should have had, threw each other around.

I didn't notice the water filling my glass prison until it was ankle deep, and despite the distraction from Atlas, those deep black eyes met mine with a smile as he tried to drown me.

I screamed, banging on the sides of my entrapment until my hands throbbed. The straggled breaths I drew into my lungs would never be enough to satiate the sheer panic. Perhaps Atlas had been right to fear the walls of the tunnels in the Storm Coven.

The confinement hadn't moved. I knew I wasn't losing space, but my mind wouldn't hear it. Wouldn't focus beyond the prison wall closing in. I shouted until my voice had gone, but there was no way Atlas could hear. Not as a burst of his wind collided with a stream of Levin's water. Atlas hadn't trained with magic. He hadn't spent his life casting in small moments just to feel the power ripple below his skin.

The water sloshed up to my waist, rising quickly as I watched Atty, that beautiful man with a mark upon his soul but true kindness in his heart, falter. Heavy arms dropped to his side, and he looked toward me with panicked eyes, seconds before Levin cast, and Atlas fell, slackened to the ground. I couldn't hear the laughter from this distance. Only see the flutter of Levin's shoulders when Atty collapsed.

Every limb threatened to buckle as tears pooled in my eyes. The tiny sliver of hope vanished when I watched him fall, absolutely gutting me. He'd fought for me, and I'd lost him because of it. I was never worthy of that sacrifice. I couldn't swallow, couldn't manage a breath, couldn't string together thoughts as helplessness devoured me. After years of running, I had nothing left.

Levin spun, menace and jubilation seeping from him in waves as he stormed across the frozen lake. "Fitting that my freedom will come on the anniversary of my damnation."

I shook my head, the water rising above my ears as I floated to the top of Atlas's sealed orb. With only a slice of air left, I couldn't help but hear Atlas' story in my mind.

Never lose the fight.

Whatever speech Levin was delivering outside of the bubble was beyond comprehension. The water muted all sounds. But Goddess be damned, I didn't want to let this man win. I'd spent years letting the fire within my soul extinguish out of fear. He'd taken more of my life than he even knew. As I had taken his, if he were to be believed.

I sucked in that final breath as the orb filled. Seconds turned into a minute of me slamming my feet and hands against the glass, trying anything to break it. Lungs burning, vision darkening around the edges. It was almost over. But only when I looked down, that tiny sleigh falling out of my pocket and drifting to the ground, did my salvation occur to me. Atty hadn't known if the orb could break. Only guessed. I cast, returning the sleigh to its original size. More than twice the length of the fucking prison.

Glass shattered around me, the water bursting outward as the sleigh landed with a crash to the ground with me falling onto it. The sound of a bone breaking jarred me, pain reverberating through my ribs. I'd lurched out of the frying pan and been tossed into the fire, it seemed. Levin snatched me from the ground, his powerful fingers gripping my throat. He wanted to suffocate me. His feelings of vengeance and vindication might have even done so if not for the abrupt snap of his neck.

Atlas.

13

"Never, ever lock someone in one of your globes again if there's even a hint of a chance that you could die or pass out or fall down and break a fucking leg." I shoved him, though it killed my ribs, and I had no idea how badly he'd been hurt.

"Marley," he said, helping me to my feet.

"And the next time you decide to sacrifice yourself and just—"

"Marley!"

"No. We're supposed to be a team and figure this—"

He didn't let me finish as he threw his arms around me, holding me so tight I could feel the heart pounding in his chest and the sheer pain within my body roaring in protest. I hissed, and he relented. Only slightly.

Checking on his emotions, the fear and relief were nearly equal. There was a fading sense of desperation and panic, and all of that combined overwhelmed me until I simply wrapped my arms around him, too, letting the reality of what had just happened wash over me.

Five years. For five years, I'd been running and hiding and spending every second of my life afraid. He'd found me so many times. I'd escaped those hands and that power by luck over and over again, knowing that one day, my luck would run out.

The tears fell as I finally let my own feelings take over. This moment wasn't about the man holding me nor the one lying dead on the ground, it was about me and my salvation. It was about gaining an ounce of my life back. And maybe I couldn't face my parents yet, but there was healing here. And there could be healing there, too.

"Okay?" he whispered.

"Mostly." I pulled away to wipe the tears, clutching my stomach.

"Are you hurt?"

"I think I broke a rib, maybe two. You?"

He moved in closer, brushing a hand over my stomach until I winced. "Just knocked the wind out of me. We better wrap this. I know a healer in the Moss Coven. We just have to rush through Forest. Think you can make the ride?"

"I wouldn't miss it."

"Good. Let's fix you up and get the hell out of here."

He snagged a blanket, drying it with his wind magic before approaching me. "I can wrap it over your clothes, but they're wet. Either I blast you with magic I can't really control to dry you, or you—"

"I have to take off my coat and shirt, don't I?"

"You're only making yourself colder because you're sopping wet. I won't look."

I fumbled for words. For air. "You can look, Atlas. Just be gentle."

He manipulated the buttons on my coat with ease, but the second I raised my arms and swore, he ripped the shirt off as fast as he could, bearing me to the elements. His eyes didn't leave mine as his knuckles brushed my skin, devouring me with the only heat I'd felt in hours.

"I'll be quick, Frostbite. Are you ready?"

I nodded, my lips quivering as I covered my chest. He didn't falter. Rushing but keeping the bandage tight. I could hear only a small breath when I moved my arms and my breasts fell free. Still, he did not look down. Even if he had, I'm not sure it would have been as intoxicating as that gaze on me.

"Better?" he whispered as soon as the fabric was tied.

"Thank you. Yes."

He dried my things, and I dressed, letting that moment replay in my head repeatedly. As much as I pleaded with my mind to focus, I could hardly manage. Even though this journey had just become far more dangerous.

But I would not let myself be afraid or weak. Not as he carefully pushed the sleigh across the top of the ice. Not as he gathered all four of our horses and brought them to me on the opposite side. Not even as the sun dropped, and the night fell bitterly cold.

"We'll have to stop," Atlas said, at last, shivering beside me. "We can't push the horses through the night."

"The water ruined their food."

"We'll restock in the Forest Coven. I have friends there. Some shifters live at the base of the summit, and they'll have food for us, too."

The ball of fire from the queen had survived through Atlas' protective barrier. But when I refused the dome over the sleigh, unable to see beyond the entrapment, he hadn't protested. Just used his wind to dry everything he could and buried us both in all the furs and blankets.

"And for tonight?" I asked, scanning the tundra of dead trees, ice and snow.

"We have to find shelter, Marley. I'll leave a door, and if it gets to be too much, you can say, and we'll try to keep going. Can you deal with that?"

Though I hated the thought, I couldn't bear the cold another second. Each shiver wracked my body with so much pain, eventually I'd pass out from it. Even with that warm ball of fire between us, it wasn't enough without something to trap the heat in.

"I'll deal with it," I managed through chattering teeth.

He cast over the horses first, explaining that they may be afraid of the magic, but their body heats would help keep them warm. I wondered why he hadn't done this the first night, but of course he hadn't. He didn't use magic unless he absolutely had to. It was not a convenience, but a hindrance to his pride. That was the fight within him, I realized. Even if he hadn't. Once he'd set his mind, that was it.

Our dome was warm within minutes, but I was chilled to the bone, and I knew it would take more than one night for me to feel anything but the muscle aches from shivering, the stabbing in my ribs, and the pang of hunger in my stomach.

When we lay down, there was no pillow between us, and we scooted together without words. For warmth, mostly, I convinced myself. Atlas brought his arms behind his head, staring up at the moon while I rested on his chest, mindful of my tender ribs.

"What was it like? Being a wolf?"

His broad chest rose and fell, the silence hanging between us. "It was like... when a witch grounds themself and they become connected to the Earth differently than we all already are. Only it's really the moon that speaks to you, calls to you. It's like feeling light surge and empower you. Like being one with everything and yet... somehow alone. Though I'm not sure if that was the wolf or the man peeking through."

"Did you lose the pack when your father kicked you out?"

"Yes," he whispered, his voice so soft I hardly heard him.

"I wonder if something in you misses having that more than you realize. If that's where the loneliness comes from."

"I have my friends. They're my pack now."

I slowly reached an arm over his chest but my ribs protested and I had to move to my back. "They're lucky to have such a loyal and decent friend."

"When Torryn pulled the short stick to go to the human lands and guard Eden, I volunteered. I've never told anyone that. He still thinks I didn't have a choice. Going there, I gave up most of what I knew, but I kept a brother safe and gained Eden's friendship. And going to the human lands, you don't know if you're going to make it home. It's dangerous to get back. It was worth it, though."

My eyes grew heavy as he spoke, the smooth tone of his voice a comfort, lulling me to sleep while he spoke the memories of his friendships out loud. But that comfort of sleep didn't last as my eyes shot open, and Present hovered above us.

14

“I don’t think the goddess would approve, witch,” Present hissed, staring at the way I laid in Atlas’ arm while we slept.. “You know he is marked.”

Looking at her was always like peering into a mirror. She looked like me, spoke like me, even mimicked my mannerisms. On my best days, it was jarring. Looking into my own face when I’d just been startled awake was a whole other beast.

“I’ve called you twice now, and you didn’t come. What is the point of this spell if it doesn’t help me, too?” I tried to keep my voice low to spare Atlas losing minutes of precious sleep.

She scoffed. “The magic is not there to help you. It’s there to help others.”

“Well, he’s the one that wanted you to come the first time. And the second time, it sure would have been helpful if you could have saved both of us.”

She spun in a circle, facing backward, though her head twisted all the way around to look at me. “Oops.”

I glared. “That’s it?”

“It’s time to go,” she said, snapping her fingers, causing Atlas to lurch forward and wake. She gave him one second to look at her distorted form before snapping again, magic yanking us to another place.

We stood in a home I'd never seen. The massive sitting room warmed, thanks to a crackling fireplace, and printed rugs matched the heavy drapes covering the windows. When I noted our reflection in the mirror on the mantle, I could see only Atlas and I, though Present hovered beside me.

"Why try to save my life if you're going to scare me to death?" he asked her.

"Entertainment, of course."

He gave the room a once over, trying and failing to lift a book from a sideboard before returning to my side. "Why does she look like me?"

I lifted a brow. "She looks like you? I see me. It must be magic."

"And you wonder why I hate magic. Tell me that's not creepy."

Before I could, the door to the home opened. I'd nearly forgotten my worry for Atlas through this experience, but as my eyes landed on Torryn, worry flooded me. And I was sure this was going to hurt.

Torryn moved to stand in front of the mirror, pulling the hat from his head. "Will you..." He placed a fist to his mouth, clearing his throat. "Andrew, I wondered if you would... no." He spun, pacing as he swept a hand forward. "I wondered if you would like to go to dinner. There. It's easy," he told himself.

When Atlas huffed a laugh beside me, I jabbed him with an elbow. "Don't laugh. He's clearly nervous."

"Andrew's a weirdo."

I rolled my eyes. "This is present day, and it seems like Torryn likes him, so have an open mind."

"So bossy," he said with a smirk as a knock sounded on the door.

Torryn checked himself one more time in the mirror, adjusting the long twists of hair that fell over his shoulders. Setting his face, he crossed the room and pulled the door open.

"Hi. Uh, hello."

"Hey, Tor," the man said, stepping into the home. "I'm sorry I can't stay longer. I have to head to guard duty, but I got your message."

"Would you like to go to dinner with me?" Torryn blurted out to Atlas' utter delight.

He covered his hand over his mouth to keep the laughter silent.

"I'm sorry. I didn't catch that," Andrew said, running thin fingers through strawberry blond hair as he smiled kindly.

"Bit nervous," Torryn said with a chuckle. "What I mean to ask is, would you like to go to dinner with me tomorrow?"

The man stepped forward, his eyes lit with happiness, and he rested his hands on Torryn's shoulders. "I would love to. Just tell me when and where."

"My place? Uh, here? I'll cook you dinner. Let's say seven-thirty?"

The men faded away as the door opened, and Present gestured for us to go outside. As we stood on the road just outside of the home, the day zipped by in a breeze. The moon trekked across the sky, the sun rose, people hurried up and down the streets, trudging through a growing blizzard. And then time slowed again as we landed in the evening. Andrew hustled up the walk toward the home, holding a bottle of something tucked under his arm.

He knocked, bouncing on his toes as he waited for Torryn to open the door. No answer. He leaned to the side, looking into a window before pulling a watch from his pocket. Again, he knocked. After the third time, he hung his head and left the house.

"See?" Atlas asked, leaning against a nearby tree. "Torryn stood him up anyway."

I shook my head. "Why would he do that? He seemed so excited."

"Changed his mind. Realized the guy's a tool."

The smile on Present's face was a little too wide as she snapped those damn fingers, and the world around us melted into the tavern where we'd first met. In fact, as I glimpsed myself across the room, I realized this was, in fact, two nights ago.

"Look at the way you're staring at me, Frostbite. Not an ounce of shame on that face."

"Focus," Present demanded, blurring the rest of the room with a wave of her hand until only Atlas and Torryn could be distinguished.

The king's message dropped from the ceiling, just as it had before. Atlas picked up the letter and read it before setting it back on the table.

"Aw, come on. Can't someone else do this?"

"He says you can do it the old-fashioned way. Go on foot if you want."

Atlas' eyes narrowed. "The old-fashioned way is gone. A foot is hardly a replacement for a paw. We both know I'll never run as a wolf again."

That sentence struck me harder hearing it again after the admissions he'd made last night.

"And I'll never fly again," Torryn said. "But there is joy in being a witch, Atty. You just have to find it."

"Magic is a damnation," he huffed. "I mean, it's not, but… you know what I mean."

Torryn pulled several long draws from his mug before resting his hands on the table to stand. Atlas protested.

"You can't leave yet, Tor. You just got here."

"I've got plans," he said, looking toward the door.

"You promised me last time you'd stay longer. I need you as a buffer for all these women."

By his tone, he'd meant it to be a joke, but it absolutely wasn't.

"Just let him go, you prick," Atlas whispered from beside me, clearly annoyed with himself.

Torryn slumped back into his seat, gesturing for another round. "Okay, Atty. I'll stay."

"And as you both know, he did." Present said, all movement slamming to a halt before she snapped her fingers.

Again, the room changed, shifting into pure white walls, a long meeting table down the middle of an opulent room. I managed a glance at Atlas to see if he knew what we'd see next, but his confusion matched my own until the door slammed open.

I couldn't help my gasp as the Dark King, wings and all, came striding into the room with his new queen trailing behind him. Maybe he'd been vindicated, and maybe he'd saved our power, but he was still intimidating, and every warning from my entire childhood had been about him.

I collided with the wall before I realized I was moving.

"Handsome, isn't he?" Present whispered in my ear.

I shook my head, looking anywhere but at the man with dark hair and silvery eyes, power pulsing from him, even now. Raven took a seat to his right, and Kirsi and Nym walked in shortly after, taking the king's left but leaving a seat in the middle.

"Are you guys having a family meeting without me?" Atlas asked.

"They cannot hear you," Present said.

"I know how it works, Ghosty," he barked in retort.

She huffed. "I am not a ghost."

"Look like a ghost, smell like a ghost, do weird ghost shit… you're a ghost."

Present glared but said nothing more.

No one in the room spoke until Torryn entered, shutting the door quietly behind him before taking the open seat directly to the Dark King's left.

"I'm listening," the king said, holding his hands in a fist before him.

"You've got to do something about Atlas," Kirsi began.

He went rigid beside me. I tried to take his hand, but he refused, steeling himself.

"He needs somebody—or something—to occupy him. He's following us around like a lost puppy. And sometimes three's a crowd," she said, sharing a look with Nym. "I love Atty, I really do. But he's driving us crazy because he cannot be alone."

If only they knew how truly lonely he felt all the time. The hurt in his eyes nearly broke me as he listened to his friends, the only companions he had in the world, speak about him as if he were only a problem to be solved.

"They're saying these things because they love you and they care for your happiness, Atty," I tried.

He couldn't hear me, though, not over Torryn's next words. "We need to give him a job. Something to keep him busy. Maybe with other people he can befriend."

"I can't believe we are having this conversation." The queen rose from her chair, shaking her wild hair as she looked them all in the eyes. "Atlas would do literally anything for any of you at the drop of a hat. It cannot be so bad that you've called a meeting."

Kirsi stood also, placing her hands flat on the table between them. "He sent spiders under our door for days until we agreed to go to the tavern with him. And not because he couldn't go by himself. Because he's afraid he's going to meet someone. We love him, too, Rave, but he's using us as a buffer for women. And to keep him busy so he doesn't have to be lonely."

The Dark King cleared his throat. "I'll ask him to gather the Yule logs for this year's Solstice."

Torryn turned in his seat. "That's a dangerous journey for him to make alone."

"It's a job that needs done. Do you want to go with him?" the king asked, lifting a dark brow.

Atlas seemed to hold his breath beside me, waiting for the answer he already knew would come. Since we were here now without the man he called a brother.

"Not particularly. But I guess we give him the task, and if he asks me to join, I'll do it."

"Don't worry, Tor. I won't," Atlas grumbled.

Present hissed a laugh as the walls faded away, and Atlas held a hard glare at his boots.

15

When I woke to a chill and rolled to find him gone, I jerked upward, pain searing my ribs as I searched beyond the glass walls of his magical dome, only to find him sitting in a bank of snow having a heart-to-heart conversation with one of the horses. I couldn't hear his words, but I could feel his sadness as if it were my own.

He'd left an opening in his magical barrier and dropped all of his blankets on me sometime in the night. Who knew how long he'd been out there? Still, he'd thought of me enough to make sure I didn't feel trapped. And that felt like progress.

I folded the blankets and stacked the pillows and furs before he noticed the movement. When he shared a forced smile and lifted from the ground, dusting the wet snow from his bottom, the horse knickered and tossed his head back, as if sad to leave their private conversation.

"Ready for this?" he asked.

"Do you want to talk ab—"

"No. They're good people, Marley, and they mean well. Let's just leave it at that."

"But Tor—"

"We've got at least one more night stuck together. As soon as Future comes and delivers her final blow, we can be done with this. Let's just let that be enough."

"Stuck together?"

His jaw tightened as he dared me to disagree. I didn't.

The ride into the Forest Coven was short, but no number of warnings could have prepared me for the onslaught of grief as we crossed that bridge. The second we passed over the spot the Harrowing had struck Laramie, the world seemed to shrink. Atlas stopped breathing.

I reached across the sleigh and took his hand. I expected him to shut me out. To push me away again. But he didn't. He gripped my fingers, his giant palms swallowing them as he closed his eyes and titled his head back.

"Just breathe, Atty."

A single tear fell, and he swallowed.

"I fucking hate this place."

"I know," I whispered, leaning my head on his shoulder as the horses carried us along the path he'd once carried her as she died in his arms. "I know."

For all the strength in those beasts' legs, the minutes dragged on as we waited for the small village in the distance to draw near, Atlas fighting a silent battle against the power those memories held over him.

"Any idea where the log is?"

"No clue."

When the horses finally stopped, I squeezed his hand. "Let me go. I can do this one."

I couldn't hold this morning against him, knowing how much he was hurting, but also confident this would all be ending soon, and maybe we both needed to be more careful. He still wasn't ready for the word 'commitment', let alone the follow through. Though broken, he remained blind to his own plight.

"I'm stronger than I look."

I forced a smile. "You look pretty strong from where I'm sitting."

He smiled, pressing his forehead to mine, and my chest constricted. "You're pretty great, you know?"

The words 'stuck together' echoed through my mind, but I had to give him space to feel, to push beyond the anger and hurt in his heart. That was the point of all of this. It wasn't about me. Not really.

"You're not too bad yourself, Wolf. Even when you're sad."

The small village didn't balk at our arrival. We could have been two random Forest Coven witches passing through town as hardly anyone paid us any mind at all.

"A year ago, they would have tried to kill me. Ten years ago, they did. And now, just because I have markings, I'm allowed to stand here. Doesn't seem right."

"Because it's not right, Atty. It wasn't right then either."

He stopped short the moment we came to the spot Laramie had fallen to the ground. "I'm grateful, you know. For the memories. No matter what kind of trouble I'm in now, or how marked or whatever it is you claim is wrong with me. I wouldn't change it. I wouldn't lose a day with her for this lifetime of misery without her."

"You?"

We turned to see a woman with white hair standing, cradling the Yule log in her arms. It took me a second to recognize her. But not Atlas. He shifted sideways, blocking me from the elder woman. Laramie's mother. The one that had screamed her hatred so loud in his memories, they were likely part of the source of that mark on his heart.

I moved around Atlas, rushing to the woman to take the log before bad turned to worse. She dropped the wood into my arms, but her cold eyes never left Atlas. Even when I hissed in pain.

"Do you remember her? My girl. Do you remember?"

"Does she want to kill me?" Atlas whispered, barely audible.

I cast toward the woman only to find a heartache as big as his and a deep well of grief and regret.

"No."

He nodded.

"You remember her stories?" The woman shuffled forward, her voice nearly inaudible.

"We were happy," he told her, taking a tentative step. "She felt love and happiness on that final day and every day before that. She loved you, too, you know? For what it's worth. She would never have left this place behind because she loved her family so much."

Unshed tears filled her eyes as she tightened the shawl draped over her shoulders and moved another step toward him. But she spoke no more, simply nodding before walking away.

"Do you think she knew you would be the one to come?" I asked as we got back in the sleigh.

He lifted a shoulder. "All this time, it seemed like everyone else just moved on with their lives as if something catastrophic hadn't happened. Because it hadn't. Not to them. But losing Laramie was like forgetting how to breathe. How to live. And I was alone with that for a long time. I bet she was, too.

"If Bash told them it would be me, she was coming either way. To kill me for the moments I'd stolen with Laramie or to share in her grief. Mourning someone is really fucking lonely, Marley."

His words seeped over me as I thought of my brother. And then my parents. I'd felt that loneliness and the guilt, but I'd never gone back to share the grief. Maybe it was time. Maybe.

16

The ride to the Moss Coven seemed as long as the whole first leg of the trip. After stopping to meet the shifters at the base of the shifter's summit to grab provisions, I could tell the journey was weighing on both of us more than we'd ever expected.

This would have been difficult for Atlas, even if he wasn't traveling the covens while at the mercy of the Spirits' power. But Future was coming, and that would be the end of all of this. Because as much as I'd witnessed the goodness of Atlas' heart, that deep dark part that damned him hadn't wavered an inch.

It took the whole day to travel to the northern tip of the Moss Coven. The dead trees and snow-covered ground hadn't changed and even though the sun still shone, it was likely as tired as we were and would set soon enough. Winter was always a blanket over our magical realm. We stopped to rest the horses and eat only when our stomachs protested the long stretch of time or my ribs ached for a break.

"Tell me something about your life. What did you do after you left Storm?" Atlas finally asked, cutting into the silence we'd curated as the hours increased our tension and my awareness of this journey's impending end. "Only if you want to, of course."

I picked at the frayed edge of the blanket over my lap. "There's not a lot to say..."

"You were seventeen when that happened?"

"I was."

"I guess losing our families gives us something in common. Does the magic only come to you before Winter Solstice?"

I nodded.

"So, what do you do for the rest of the year?"

"Avoid people as much as possible. I travel around a lot. I work with a few Whisper Coven witches transporting wine to the other covens. It's not lucrative, but I eat and usually find shelter."

He settled in, finally resting against the seatback. "Usually?"

"Well, I've been on the run from Levin for five years. It's harder to hunt someone when you can't nail them down to one spot. I'm guessing someone from the Storm Coven let him know we were coming to River."

"That fucking guard." Atlas clinched a fist around the reins.

"Probably. It's easy to pay off a starving witch."

"Things are going to get better for everyone. Trade is a good idea, Frostbite. The covens just have to learn to trust each other again." He wrapped an arm around my shoulders. "We should talk to Bash about it when we get home."

Home.

The word plummeted in my gut like an anvil. I didn't have a home. I hadn't had one for a very long time, and the thought of being tied down to a single place stopped appealing to me the second I was on my own. But sitting next to Atlas, a constant companion these past days, made something in me wonder if my heart was missing out. If I could settle and be happy doing anything but running.

"I'll think about it."

"That sounds very uncommital," he said with a roguish grin.

"That's not even a word, Wolf."

"Unspirited?"

"Pretty sure that's also not a word."

"It really is. And it's true."

Resting in the crook of his arm, I looked at the trees that accompanied us as we made our way through the snow-laden trail. "I never said I was perfect. I have my own demons."

He pulled the horses to a stop as he turned and placed a finger under my chin to force my gaze to his. "Demons are meant to be slayed."

"That sounds very committal," I whispered.

He leaned his forehead against mine. "Baby steps."

As I gave the command to continue down the snowy path, my heart hammered in my chest.

Could he? Could we?

It was too fragile of a time to consider the possibilities of a future beside this man. I'd seen these things time and time again. Some would change, some would not. And no matter how much hope I'd had from afar, it never seemed to change me.

Because I was a hypocrite. I'd been one since the day my brother died. Maybe my heart was not marked the same way Atlas' was, but there was still damage done.

"Have you ever seen anything like this in Moss?" Atlas asked, nudging me with his shoulder as he stepped around from the back of the sleigh, closing our blankets into the boxes.

"Never," I answered, mouth agape from taking in the music and laughter from a festival happening in the heart of the village.

Small children circled the thick skirts of their mothers as the gathering grew in volume. Chatter filled the square, overtaking the lively music coming from the witches dressed in furs as they swung ribbons through the air in celebration.

"Let's go see if we can find Eden Mossbrook, huh?"

"*The* Eden Mossbrook?"

He wiggled his eyebrows. "The one and only. Bash told her I was coming with one of his little love notes, I'm sure."

"Is that..." I narrowed my eyes.

"What?"

"Is that jealousy I hear in your voice?"

"Psh. No. Magical letters are not that appealing."

I hid my grin as he tugged me into the throng of people dancing in the village square, laughing and singing off key as the music surrounded us.

With smiles abundant, I couldn't believe this was the coven of Endora Mossbrook, the most feared and dangerous of the coven leaders. But as a woman approached us, with half white and half black hair and stunning opposite eye colors, I couldn't help but see the reason behind it. Not as she yanked Atlas from my hand, gripping him into a hug when he lifted her and spun her around.

He set her down, and she reached forward, messing up his hair, that beautiful smile never wavering. "I've missed you, Pup."

"About time someone did."

She pulled away, searching his eyes for more than what his words conveyed, before yanking him into another hug. Only then did she see me, standing awkwardly close, watching the exchange.

"Who's your friend?"

"Oh." Atty winked at me. "This is Marley. Marley, this is Eden, Mother-Slayer, Mossbrook."

"Atlas," she chided, shoving him away. "Don't say it like that."

"It's nice to meet you," I said, sheepishly, staring at the woman that had been hunted far longer than I was.

"Any chance you can take a look at her ribs?"

She narrowed her eyes. "What did you do, Atlas?"

He took a step back, showing his palms. "Calm down, slayer. It wasn't me. We ran into a little trouble."

She moved closer to me, hovering her hand just above my wound. "I hope nothing serious. May I?"

"Please," I managed, still in awe of the woman.

She closed the space, pressing along my ribs until I winced. "There," she said softly, the marking on her neck glowing green as she cast and light filled me.

Within seconds, I could take a full breath. In less than a minute, I could stand straight. Atlas stared at us, his eyes pinned to the spot Eden held until she pulled away.

"Better?"

I moved closer to Atty, nodding. "Yes. Thank you very much."

She looked down at my red fingers. "It's warmer by the fires."

"It's also warmer if you're moving," Atlas cut in, grabbing my hand, and pulling me into the crowd of witches. "One dance won't kill our timeline, right, Frostbite?"

I shook my head with a grin as he dipped his chin to Eden before swinging me around. "I'll come find you in a few," he yelled over his shoulder.

"Some people never change, Atlas," she shouted back.

He stared down at me, swiping a snowflake from my cheek. "Some people."

My brain didn't want to believe the promise behind those words, but my heart sure did. Especially with his body flush to mine.

"Are you ready?" he asked, sliding a hand firmly around me.

"I don't know."

Sweat had already begun forming on my palms, doubt creeping in as I tried and failed to remember the last time I'd danced with someone.

He tucked a finger beneath my chin and lifted. "Don't look down. Eyes on me."

"I'm afraid I'm going to trip you."

He leaned his head to mine. "Trust me, okay?"

I didn't have time to answer as the music began once more, sweeping us away as we circled the ground, each step taking us closer to the point of no return. Two fast songs melted into something more slow and haunted, but Atlas never missed a beat. Never took his eyes from me as he carried us around the open space, forgetting his mention of one dance.

He was still a wolf. No matter what ability he'd lost or how bare it must have felt for him to lose that core sense of himself, he still had the innocence of a wild animal and the loyalty of a shifter. These past days had been curated to destroy him. To rip everything he knew about himself apart and leave him open, aching for something better than the life he lived now. But as he held me, thumb stroking the small of my back while we swayed and spun, lost in each other, I knew without checking that mark, the goddess' minions would never break his spirit. The wild wolf with a mischievous grin would always be a dangerous thing for a heart to bet on.

"You shouldn't look at me like that," I breathed.

A growl deepened his voice. "You're right, I shouldn't."

Atlas grabbed the back of my neck and pulled my lips to his. We stopped moving. The entire world paused, everything losing all sense of color and vibrancy compared to the way my heart yearned for that broken man. He slipped his tongue into my mouth and groaned, my knees weakening enough that he gripped me tighter.

I knew this was dangerous territory, but, still, I let my magic slip, reaching for him, praying desperately I would find anything beyond the lust within his feelings.

But something locked me out. I couldn't see a single emotion. Only blackness. In a panic, I pulled away, casting to the nearest witch.

Happiness.

"What's wrong?" he asked, suddenly alert and scanning the crowd as I had been.

"N-nothing. It's nothing."

"Are you sure?" His eyes searched mine for more.

"Just got a little dizzy. Do you mind if we find something to drink? Maybe we should get the Yule log and head back to the sleigh. We still have to go to Whisper."

He hesitated, still studying my face. "We have a full day to get to Whisper and then to the castle. I'm not in a hurry, are you?"

I shook my head. I wasn't. Not at all.

"Good."

He led us out of the crowd to a small table with green ribbons hanging to the ground and two little girls keeping watch over a pitcher of water.

"May I?" Atty asked, gesturing to the small cups.

"Momma says it's good practice for us to pour and serve our neighbors," one of them answered.

"Well then, I would be most honored to have such a well-mannered young lady serve me and my friend."

The smaller one giggled as the first tried to curtsy before lifting the heavy pitcher. As soon as the water splashed into the cup, it tilted to the side and spilled. When the little girl's big, brown eyes filled with tears, Atlas moved to a knee, committing to get his pants muddy to steady the girl.

"I've always found this part tricky," he said calmly, righting the cup. "This is a two-man job, if ever I've seen one. Shall we try again?"

She smiled through her tears and grabbed the pitcher. With two successful cups poured, the other girl holding the second as Atty instructed her, we turned to leave. But he stopped mid-stride, reaching into his pocket and pulling out two coins.

"Have you ever had a coin before?" he asked the girls.

They both shook their heads, eyes locked on the copper between his fingers.

"These are special coins from a special friend of mine." He dropped one into each of their waiting hands. "The new queen is lovely. If you take these to the castle when you visit for Solstice, and tell the gatekeeper Atlas sent you, they will know you're there to meet her."

One girl blushed, and the other giggled. "Will the Dark King be there too?"

"Would that scare you?"

The girl that had spilled the water straightened her spine before shaking her head. "I'm not afeared of him anymore."

"Because you're brave," I said, smiling down at her. "And smart."

She nodded before turning to her next customer.

"You're kind of incredible," I said when we slipped away.

Atlas lifted his eyebrows. "Shh. People will hear you."

I giggled. "I'm serious."

As we chatted, I noticed the crowd around us parting. At first, I thought maybe to avoid the man that had once been a shifter, but it wasn't that. They were women. All of them were staring at him as he stared at me. I knew it would only be a matter of time, but my heart was not ready when one of them stepped forward and plucked up the courage to ask for a dance.

17

The beautiful witch with sweeping black hair and piercing green eyes stared up at Atlas until he readily agreed, handing me his empty water cup as he swept her into the crowd of dancers. Something within me burned when he leaned down to whisper, making her laugh and toss her head back, swatting his chest. I turned, unable to watch.

Instead, I dropped the cups on the table beside the little girls and pushed back through the gathering, thinking I'd wait for him in the sleigh. But when Eden stopped me, I couldn't be rude and refuse her company. Not to a woman that had healed me moments ago.

"You can't take it personally," she said, looking through the people until her eyes fell on Atlas. "He's got a history, and it's something that's haunted him for a long time. But he's worth the wait if you have the patience he'll need."

"I know, and I don't take it personally," I answered, my tone far more bitter than I'd intended. "We're just friends. Like he said."

"I believe that to be true for him, but I think you feel differently."

"I should go," I said, walking away, her opinion of me be damned.

Because he was worth it, and fuck me if I couldn't keep my heart from seeing the potential. He would always be the nice guy everyone pined over and no one nailed down. He hadn't batted an eye when that witch asked him to dance. Hadn't considered me for a second. I couldn't see the change in him because there was none.

"You're beautiful when you're jealous."

Atlas' voice cut across the temper-filled silence like a knife. It didn't matter how far behind us the Moss Coven celebration had been, not when he consumed the world with simple words.

I placed a foot into the sleigh and lifted myself up before looking back at him. "I'm not jealous."

"No?"

He took several strides forward. "Feelings aren't just measured by magic, Marley. I can see it written on your face." Another step. "I can see it in the way you reach for my hand." Another. "And the way you smile." He gripped the sides of the sleigh, placing one boot between my legs to hoist himself until he was inches from me. "I can see it in the way you look at me." An inch closer. "And the way you hold your breath when I speak to you."

I opened my mouth to protest, but he closed the space, his burning lips on mine until my back pressed against his glass barrier on the opposite side. Firm hands gripped my waist as every single wall between us came crashing down.

"Tell me you don't want this," he demanded, burying a hand into my hair to force my gaze to his. "Tell me you don't want me."

I tried and failed to catch my breath as he waited for an answer.

"I do want this."

He kissed me again, so fervently, so thoroughly, if not for the hand on my waist, I might have melted to the floor. Every part of me came alive at his touch as he pressed his body to mine, lifting my arms above my head and pinning them to his magical wall while he devoured me.

Hot fingertips graced my stomach when he untucked my shirt and slid a palm beneath my clothing, causing my flesh to tingle and tighten.

"Can I have you? All of you?"

I nodded, not giving a damn about the glass walls or the fact that, while we may have been hidden down the road a little way, it wasn't nearly far enough to keep the celebration goers from seeing us, should they come traipsing down the trail to their homes.

His lips purred against my throat as he whispered, "With your words, Marley."

"All of me," I managed.

"Good girl," he said, seconds before his free hand dipped below my waistband.

I couldn't concentrate on any of it. Not his tiny kisses down my neck, not the fingers brushing my thighs as he teased me. Not the firm hand holding mine hostage against the wall. He was explosive in the best way, overwhelming my senses as I tasted him and touched him. Felt him and heard those groans as he explored me.

He dropped my hands to rip his shirt over his head and pressed his heated chest against me. I could feel the broken heart thundering within him. I moaned the second my fingers grazed his muscled back, and he traced a finger down my core.

I cast, unraveling his pants as he gripped my shirt and tugged it off. Sucking in a sharp breath, I covered myself long enough to check our surroundings.

"Worried someone will see us?" The mischievous glint in his eyes faltered as the last of his pants transformed into a pile of thread on the floor.

"Not hardly."

His lopsided grin was my complete undoing. Wearing only his boots, it might have been comical if his body hadn't been built into something god-like. My tongue darted across my lips as I let my eyes drink him in.

"It should be a sin to die without ever seeing someone so fucking perfect," he said, moving his thumb over a hardened nipple.

Every inch of my body heated for him. To even stand before his hungry gaze lit me on fire.

"Pants off," he ordered, hooking a finger through a belt loop. "Before I rip them off myself."

He turned feral in those moments. No longer a chivalrous man, the beast within him had surfaced, and I was all in, kicking off my boots and dropping my pants, bearing myself for the world to see, should anyone bother. And if they did, I hoped it turned them on as much as he did me.

Sliding his fingers between my legs again, he pulled them away, licking them as he fell backward onto the bench. "Come here, Frostbite."

He gripped himself at the base, waiting for me.

"Say please," I answered.

He brushed a thumb over his lip, eyes dropping before the word 'please' left his mouth in a guttural beg.

Stepping out of my pants, I moved close enough for Atlas to reach forward and stroke between my legs as he stared up at me. At first, it was just a heavy breath at his touch, but one turned into two until I was panting from the way he traced his fingertips along my slick entrance. Playing long before he would deliver the pleasure I needed so desperately.

"Say please," he said, mimicking my prior command. His voice rippled down my spine.

But I could play, too. I inched backward, daring him to repeat himself. He was off the bench in an instant, kissing me soundly before shaking his head at me.

"Do you want me to make you beg?"

My back pressed against the cold barrier, and I gasped as he lifted me, spreading my legs so that I hovered just about him.

"Say please," he growled.

He waited at my opening, the tip of him brushing against me as he stared into my face, daring me to refuse him. I relaxed my shoulders, thinking I could wiggle down just enough to make him change his mind. But it only made the longing worse. Atlas lowered me entering halfway with a gasp before he lifted my thighs, pulling out, the strain in his voice uninhibited as I groaned.

"Say please, or I'll put you down and make you watch me handle it myself."

The thought alone was my undoing as I gave in. "Please," I whispered, the word leaving my lips as if I had no true control.

"Good girl," he growled before thrusting as he lowered me onto him again.

He was glorious. Every inch. Everything about him. I dug welts into his back as I held on, letting him slam me into the barrier as he moved, holding my gaze the entire time. The glass fogged over long before he was done. His muscles never strained as he worked, watching me with feral intent until I thought I might burst beneath those icy blue eyes. The pool of desire within me peaked beyond the point of no return, and just when I thought I'd shatter around him, he stopped. Those desperate thrusts paused as he held me upright for a beat before pulling out and setting me down gently.

"Not like this," he said between rapid breaths, ashy hair falling into his face.

I stood wide-eyed, wondering what had happened in that beautiful mind of his as he turned and moved the blankets to the floor.

"Lay here."

"There's hardly room for this."

"There's enough. I promise."

Sandwiched between the wall and the bench, he was right. Though only just.

He hovered above me, brushing my hair from my face while staring. I felt so bare beneath that gaze. As if I stood naked before the entire world.

"Don't," he said as I looked away. "Eyes on me."

I couldn't help but cater. The second our eyes locked, he thrust, burying himself to the hilt before pulling all the way out and kissing me. Back and forth he went. Slow and steady, rocking the sleigh as he moved but keeping a perfect cadence. A kiss and a glorious drive, over and over. Until my body anticipated every movement. My muscles tightened. Building and building as everything grew hotter and our bodies slicker. Until the strain of holding myself together was more than I could stand. Until I wanted to come out of my skin for need of release.

I whimpered.

"Just like that," he said. "Let me fucking hear you."

Every part of my body clenched around him as I squeezed my eyes shut, screaming his name.

"Say it again," he ordered, still pushing in and out as I trembled around him. "Tell me how good it feels, Marley."

"Atlas," I moaned. "So, so..."

My voice trailed off as he chuckled and slammed forward again, stealing my descent, and forcing me to rise again, each thrust, each heartbeat his and his alone. My aching muscles tightened again.

"One more time," he managed, though far more strained. "Let me watch you come undone for me."

The world fell away. My sight entirely gone as he burst the same moment I fell from that mountain he'd taken me to the top of. And as I fell, I watched his face. Pleasure stolen as he looked down upon me with something new in his eyes.

Fear, the magic seemed to whisper.

He seized. I reached for him. He moved away.

"Atlas?"

"You were perfect," he said. "You've been perfect since the moment you fell into my arms."

But those words were not a compliment. Simply my damnation as he stood, dressing above me before mumbling about needing to get the log from Eden and practically running from the sleigh.

When I sat up, gathering the furs to cover my heated skin, I'd never felt so rejected and so alone in my whole life. How the hell could he flip that switch so suddenly?

My throat burned as the tears threatened to come. I knew better. I'd known this entire time and still leapt off that mountain with him. Chest tightening, I forced our memories, that lopsided grin and the way he looked at me from my mind.

I dressed quietly, embracing the sorrow as I waited for him to return, hoping he just needed to catch his breath. But minutes turned into hours as I stared into that magical ball of fire heating the dome, and I wondered what I should do.

Surely, he hadn't run too far. He knew what would happen. But as I stared at that village in the distance, as the celebration slowly came to an end, I realized I'd been used. And I knew it. I'd set myself up for this moment, and I couldn't even blame him for what I knew he wasn't ready for.

I wished I could have run. Let him come back and find me gone. But I was stuck. If we got too far apart, Death would come for him. And no matter how upset I was, I wouldn't wish that finality upon him. His soul was good, even his heart was good. Mark or no mark, he was everything. Until he wasn't.

I didn't notice the ominous hooded figure floating before me until the sleigh faded away.

Fuck.

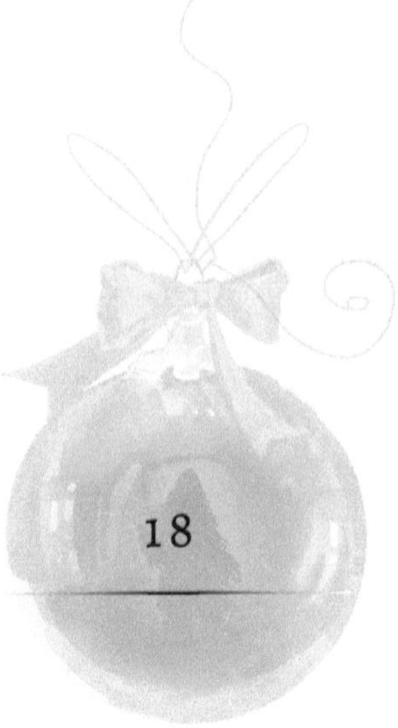

18

"Fuck."

Atlas' voice was the first and last thing I wanted to hear. But it was time to pay the piper, and Future had come at last, her mysterious face still hidden within the confines of her hood, shadows billowing beneath her. I only needed to endure whatever we would see or whatever her test would be, and then I could run. Far, far away and never look back.

"Marley?" I could feel those eyes on me as he whispered my name, the tiny sound echoing off the walls of an empty dark room.

"You need to focus on Future right now, Atlas. These next moments will determine your whole life."

"We need to talk."

"No. We don't. I knew better." I spun, searching for Future's figure, but she was gone.

It took him three massive strides to get to me, to tower over me and make me feel so damn small. He opened his mouth to speak, but before a single word could leave those beautiful lips, a graveyard appeared around us. Each frosty headstone was lit dimly by the sliver of the moon nearly lost in the sky.

I swallowed the lump in my throat as Future's robed shoulder brushed mine, a bony finger pointing straight ahead to five cloaked figures surrounding a freshly dug grave.

Witches held funeral pyres, but shifters buried their dead.

Atlas slowly peeled his gaze from me, walking over to stand next to himself, studying the aged faces of the others.

"Torryn? Tor's not here."

Without a word, Future's finger lowered, pointing to the fresh grave. The ominous gesture raised the flesh on my arms as Atlas stumbled backward. He spun in a circle, staring at his friends and then beyond at the scattered graves. The empty space void of a crowd. Of anyone that Torryn might have built a life with. Because that was key. Future's sickening point. Atlas would ultimately be responsible for Torryn's loneliness.

My breaths grew short, a sharp pain growing in my chest.

"Bash? Why aren't there more people here?"

Future-Atlas knelt beside the grave, digging a hand into the small dirt pile and tossing it over the body wrapped in furs at the bottom of the pit.

"All in. All out. I'll see you there," he whispered, his voice broken.

When he stood, I realized something was different. Off. He hadn't been close enough to the others. Had distanced himself from them, choosing to stand on the opposite side of the grave, several paces away.

"No!" Atlas barked, walking over to shove his future self, though his hands did not make contact. "He was alone, you selfish bastard. Why couldn't you see it?"

The Dark King's voice covered Atlas' as he dropped his handful of dirt and said, "To the man who held so many important roles in my life. To the friend and the father he'd been to me.

To the brother and the council. May you rest in paradise. I'll see you there."

My heart wrenched in my chest hearing those gutting words.

"It shouldn't be like this." Queen Raven tucked her graying hair behind an ear as she released a handful of dirt. "I'm sorry you were alone that night. When you said you weren't feeling well, I should have stayed."

"It's not your fault, Rave," Kirsi said. "I think we all thought him to be invincible. The gentle giant that would never fall. I guess we were all wrong. I just hope we were enough for him. And that he didn't feel so alone."

Raven nodded, dusting off her hands. "I'll see you there."

Kirsi and Nym shuffled forward, gripping more dirt and releasing it at the same time.

"As above, so below. I'll see you there," they said in unison.

My soul ached for this small group of friends. I'd never had that. I wasn't sure if I hurt more because of the reality of my own loneliness, the wolf that had turned his back to everything, or the way he hung his head, likely wracked with guilt.

"It's not your fault." I walked carefully toward him, the sounds of the sniffles in the background muffling my footsteps in the snow. "At the end of the day, it was always his choice."

I could feel Future's fingers wrap around the ends of my hair as she tugged.

"It is his fault," she rasped. "He could have seen beyond himself and let his friend go find happiness, and instead, he chose to take advantage of Torryn's loyalty. Do not speak against the lessons to be learned, or I will take everything from you, Marley Stormborn."

I didn't miss the jaw tick from Atlas as he balled his hands and moved toward the ruthless Spirit.

"If you want me to change this, then just tell me how. Isn't that the purpose of this fucked up magic? To traumatize me in a different way than my life has? You didn't like how I was dealing with my past, so you're fucking with my future? Is that the plan here? I'm done with these games. I'm not afraid of you. Just tell me what you want or leave me the fuck alone. I was just fine before you came."

The gasp on my lips was hardly audible. He'd challenged Future, and that final sentence might have damned him.

"And why is Marley here? Why are you dragging her through this? She's been a pawn in your games for years and almost died because of it. Did you know that? You throw her into the hands of people you know to be terrible and then leave her to her own mercy. Binding her to them because you know her heart is too good to let them run off and fucking die."

"Atlas," I warned.

But it didn't matter as the scene around us melted away and reappeared. The snow melted. The ground covered in frost changed into a fresh pile of dirt covering a new grave we stood upon.

"What are you showing me this time, Spirit? More of my own demise?"

When my eyes traced over the headstone, I stumbled back, ice settling in my veins. Two figures, men I'd never seen before, stood leaning on shovels as they stared down at the ground. One clean cut with markings and the other unmarked. Shifter, maybe.

"I fucking hate it when they die in winter," the witch said, wiping his runny nose down a disgusting sleeve.

"This one didn't even need a plot," the other answered. "No one came."

"Did you search him? Anything good?"

The unshaven man shook his head. "Not a coin on him. Not even a brass button."

"Shoulda known."

"I know that's my name," Atlas said quietly. "But you'll never convince me that my family never came."

"Your family is chosen, not kin born of your blood." Future's voice was a hiss of poison. "Even forged bonds can be broken with enough strain. Or resentment. Or…" She twisted, pointing to Torryn's worn grave. "… guilt."

Atlas ran strong fingers through his hair as the two gravediggers hobbled away. "How can a man control a mark on his heart he never wanted?"

The second Future's attention fell on me, my breath caught in my throat.

I tried shifting behind Atlas, but she circled, the withered ends of her tattered black robes grazing the frozen ground.

Though she spoke to Atlas, her words were like a knife to my heart. "You must choose to forget. Everything. Laramie. Your parents. Your friends… Marley. If you've truly learned something from my sisters, you will not need the memories. Your soul will reset, and the mark on your heart will vanish. You will be free to create a fresh path. Untainted."

Something in my chest broke as he spun, eyes locking with mine for only a second before I could read the writing on the wall. He'd never choose to forget them. He'd said as much. And if he did, I'd be a lost memory. This was the end for us either way.

"So damned if I do, and damned if I don't." He looked up at the gray sky before shaking his head, his voice breaking."We both knew how this was going to end, Marley, didn't we?"

I nodded, dragging a frozen breath into my lungs, if only to make sure I was still breathing.

"I'm sorry," he whispered.

19

There was nothing. Only sadness and an unfamiliar awareness of my own grief. Something I'd been running from for longer than I could remember. Every muscle in my body grew heavier as the world appeared around me. One moment I was staring into those sad eyes and the next, I was alone. Again. Standing before a frosted window, looking down upon a blizzard waging war through the Fire Coven.

I couldn't look at the chair by the fire without thinking of him. Of the way he'd slumped into that seat, searching for answers after I'd damned him. I'd been whisked back to the inn he'd taken me to, and if the snowfall was an indication, I wasn't leaving anytime soon.

Tiny steps carried me to the edge of the bed before I sat heavily with the weight of the world on my shoulders. I could do this. Had done this every year for ten years at Winter Solstice. I simply needed to walk away. Because he was right, and we'd both known how it was going to end. He ran from me last night. Afraid of what he saw when he looked at me, and I deserved better than that. I just needed to convince my heart. But then, I'd always been a runner, too.

Three solid knocks on the door whisked me from despair, and I let a sliver of hope inch its dangerous way into my heart. Steeling my nerves, I swung the door open, not to find a lopsided grin, but simply the innkeeper balancing a tray.

"You haven't left this room in days, Miss. I thought maybe you could use refreshment. Tea?"

But he'd seen me leave. Had watched Atlas and I load everything onto that giant sleigh right outside of his inn.

"Please, sir. What day is it?"

Had we gone back in time somehow? Had the Spirits' magic truly been that powerful?

The scraggly man's head drew back as he scrutinized me over the question. "Tomorrow's Winter Solstice."

I hadn't missed a day. I wondered if the world had really tilted, or if I'd stumbled.

"You okay, Miss?"

"Fine. I'm fine. I'm uh… Storm Coven witch and—"

"Ah. Yes. The blizzard."

I slid my hands beneath his metal tray, if only to end the awkward silence that followed his questioning gaze.

Those fucking Spirits were probably hiding in this very room, silently cackling at my inability to adjust to their intrusive magic. Assholes.

"Th- thank you so much. This was very kind." I hooked my foot behind the door, ready to slam it shut the second he backed far enough out of the frame.

"They say the storm's likely to pass soon. The festival is still planned for—"

"I'm so sorry. I'm not feeling well. Thank you again for the gesture."

His mouth hung ajar, but he let the door shut regardless. Setting the tray down, I eyed a biscuit for less than a second before my stomach turned. I wasn't hungry, only miserable, gutted even.

I snapped the dusty curtains together, blocking out the light, the storm, the entire world as I crawled into bed and buried my head beneath the covers. If I closed my eyes and breathed slowly enough, I could feel him there, lying beside me, heating me in a way that only he, the wolf, could. I didn't blame him for saving his soul. I only blamed my heart for not protecting mine.

When my eyes closed, I saw the careful planes of his face. The deep hollow of his cheeks. The lopsided grin. The scar. Time would steal the details. Smoothing the edges of my memories so he would be nothing more than a passing thought. Except for those eyes. They'd been burned into my very being, and, as long as I lived, I'd never see anything more stunning. The eyes of a wolf, trapped in the body of a witch.

As each memory played through my mind, I thought of his misery. And then of the lightness he would feel when everything was gone. I wondered if he'd find his happiness. His friends.

I gasped so quickly I choked on air, jerking straight out of bed again. His friends. Running to the window, I ripped the curtains open. Their squealing protest against the rod at the top was hardly audible over the pounding of my own heart.

Atlas may have forgotten everything, but I remembered. They must have as well. And if he disappeared, they'd never stop searching for him. There were few things I had that much faith in, but his conviction when he spoke of his friends as if they were family, even when they'd said things that likely hurt him, was unwavering. Maybe we could help him remember.

But another fucking blizzard was wreaking havoc on the Fire Coven. I had no idea how far away the castle was, and only a vague memory of how we'd gotten there in the sleigh. I had to try, though. Should I be buried in a snowdrift and frozen through, at least I'd tried. If not for him, then for me. Because maybe he ran that night, but I was a hunter.

"YOU'RE SURE, MISS MARLEY? IT'S DANGEROUS. THEY SAY THE outside covens may not make it in time for Solstice if the storms don't settle soon."

I shoved my arm through the third layer of borrowed clothing and nodded to the innkeeper. "I'm sure. And I'll follow the directions the best I can. How much for that?"

The burly man looked over his shoulder at the long, red tapestry.

"Will you promise to bring it back?"

"On my power as a witch."

"Take it, then. It's no use to me if you have a better need."

"Precautionary." I waved a hand, letting magic rejuvenate me as the storm pulsed outside, giving me a boost I didn't need. The banner shrank to the size of a handkerchief, and I shoved it in my pocket.

"And if I don't see you in a day or two?" he asked, wringing his hands with worry.

I plopped four coins onto the counter. "Then the room is paid for."

He swiped the money and hobbled his way around to take my hands. "It's not the coin I'm worried about. You're a good tenant, to be sure. Hardly knew you were up there, but Atlas would have my hide if he knew I let you go traipsing off into this storm."

He remembered Atlas. Thank the goddess. He remembered.

"Should that ever become a problem, I will tell him you insisted I stay, and I had to sneak away."

He pressed the coins back into my hand. "Should that man turn up here looking for you, I'm afraid it will be too late for all of that. Keep the coins. There's a cabin halfway between this village and the castle, nestled into a line of dead trees. That's

Bertie's place. She's a mean, old coot, but she'll give you shelter and a hot meal for these."

I didn't plan on stopping, but the careful way his face wrinkled between his bushy brows told me he'd only find peace with a half-hearted promise.

20

"Follow the snow-covered gap between the buildings until you make it out of the village," the innkeeper had told me.

Sound advice unless the storm was too powerful and you couldn't see beyond the stretch of your own arm. In a blizzard, it doesn't matter how much snow is falling when the wind and moisture swallow the details of the world. I had an extraordinarily strong sense of direction thanks to my hunting endeavors, but even that skill was lost to the fury of nature.

As I trudged through snow as deep as my knees and drifts that could bury me, it wasn't long until I knew I should have waited. I could have given it a day and started fresh in the morning. But my heart wouldn't let me sit in that inn, picturing Atlas wandering the world, lost and alone. No matter my plight in this blizzard, his was likely worse.

Most of my Solstice hunting was done while traveling through snow and always in the cold winter, but I'd never walked through a blizzard that tried to erase the world as if something had infuriated the goddess and she was showing her wrath.

I tried to keep a straight line of footprints behind me, but within four or five paces, they were filled in. The world had been swallowed by white, wind whipping and ice forming on my frozen lashes. There were no trees. No visible landmarks at all, and though I'd wrapped myself in layer after layer, exposing only my eyes, the chill had set in.

Hours into the day, I thought maybe the storm had finally relented. The cold no longer bit as hard, the wind seemed to silence, and the muscles in my legs felt as if they worked a little less. Only when I realized that I'd become numb to everything around me, including my own self-awareness, did the worry set in. There was no end in sight. I'd never be able to see a pearly white castle in the distance, no matter how close I came. It could have been right beside me, and I'd have never known.

Eventually, the goddess—and whatever war she raged—won, and I could no longer move. I could not force a single step more. I collapsed into a snowdrift, nearly burying myself. Struggling to move, constricted from the layers of clothing and protest of my body, it took several tries before I could get the innkeeper's tapestry from my pocket and cast to make it large again, covering me in bright red like a blanket. I thought maybe the insulation from the snow would warm me enough to push onward. But as my eyes refused to battle one second more, as icy lashes fell upon frozen cheeks, the universe won, and I'd likely die frozen and alone.

Always alone.

THE LIGHT OF THE FULL MOON KISSED MY CHEEKS, DRAWING SOME kind of fight out of my exhausted body as the sound of fabric snapping yanked me back to a world determined to send me to an early pyre. Blurred vision gave only a hint of a large, masculine figure standing over me.

The storm had passed. Or so the mirage would have me believe as I blinked and brought frozen fingers to my eyelids, trying desperately to clear the blur. He was there. Rimmed in moonlight. And maybe I couldn't see the lines of his face or the details that made him beautiful. But those eyes twinkled with starlight, reaching into my chest and ripping my heart to pieces.

I couldn't save him. I hadn't saved myself, either. Only the brink of death would deliver such a cruel and desperate vision.

My heart had conjured Atlas.

"Go away," I croaked, though my voice was hardly a whisper, the edges of my sight turning black as oblivion threatened to steal me once more.

The red fabric snapped again, wrenching me into reality as I waited for the man I'd failed to fade away.

"Trust me, Frostbite. You don't really want me to do that."

The smooth tone of his voice was echoed as if he stood at the end of a long corridor, speaking only loud enough for the world to carry those words to the tips of my consciousness.

I couldn't feel a single limb as brawny arms reached around my numb body and lifted me. Forcing my eyes open, the man turned into the moonlight, stopping my heart from beating.

"Are you real?" I whispered.

Atlas leaned his forehead on mine, closing his eyes and taking a deep, resounding breath. "I sure hope so."

My teeth chattered together as I tried to make sense of it all. "You remember me?"

"How many times have I told you to trust me?" He crushed me to his chest, though there was no warmth to be found. "You're freezing, Marley. You tried to cross this territory in the middle of a fucking blizzard. There's... someone holding the storm at bay, but we need to get you some place warm immediately. Ask questions later."

I jerked. "Who's holding the storm?"

"Later," he growled.

With little effort, Atlas lifted me to the back of a horse and mounted behind me, his firm body and the friction between us helping to bring a semblance of warmth. The breeze from the trot should have chilled me more, but I'd convinced myself I'd never truly be warm again and likewise would never feel the cold.

EDEN, WHO HAD BEEN SUMMONED TO THE CASTLE UNDER ATLAS' very watchful eye, had somehow found a way to warm me, starting from my toes and moving all the way to the top of my head. She'd been kind and thorough, but as Atlas paced the room, the questions of how this moment came to be still sat with me. And though it'd been hours within the castle, he'd still said nothing.

When Eden insisted I needed my rest and the room finally emptied, Atlas snuck back in. Standing at the edge of the bed, he massaged my feet as he stared down at me.

"I'm sorry," he said simply. "I never got the chance to say it before Future sent you away, but I am. I've spent so much time running. And I don't know. I saw the way you were watching me, and I wanted it, Marley. All of it. Late mornings in bed and holding your hand. Sunsets and holidays. I wanted inside jokes. I wanted to be the reason you smiled every single day. I wanted to never blink again, out of fear you'd disappear one day. That's why I've clung so tightly to my friends. Because if they are with me, they'll never leave me."

"They will never leave you because they love you."

"Past trauma is a sleeping beast. Sometimes, you forget it's there, and sometimes, you're running with fangs on your heels."

I felt those words in my soul as images of my brother's youthful face swirled in my mind.

"Will you tell me what happened?"

He cleared his throat, the serious look on his face melting into humor. "I was born one cold, blustery night. You're familiar with the kind."

I launched a pillow at his face, glaring. "I don't want your life story, prick. And don't use jokes to deflect. I want to know how you're here and how you remember everything. And how you found me."

He flashed that lopsided grin as he picked up the pillow from the floor and tossed it onto the bed beside me before kicking off his boots and jumping in.

"It's because I'm roguishly handsome. The Spirits took one collective look at this face and just decided they couldn't go through with their side of the bargain."

Rolling to my side, I jabbed his ribs with an elbow. "I'm serious, Atlas."

He turned to face me, tucking a finger under my chin. "The hows are not important."

"They are to me."

"Okay," he conceded. "But consider this a bedtime story. You have to rest if you want to come to Solstice, and it's already almost midnight."

"Deal," I said, staring into his searing eyes. "I don't care about Solstice, anyway."

"Future never cast upon me. According to her, I only had to agree to forget everything. I didn't lose a single memory. The act of choosing was the final test."

"Okay, so that's it? You just walked away from it?"

"Not exactly. There was paperwork, of course, a formal meeting with the goddess, the traditional gift giving ceremony, some random thing they needed some handsome beast blood for, but otherwise, that was it."

I gasped. "They took your blood?"

He leaned in with a smirk. "No, Marley. It was a joke. Present showed up to tell me you were near death in the blizzard, and I used a door Bash leaves for Eden to get to the castle. I've always been a fan of those doors."

I couldn't help my smile. "You're such a liar. You refused to use them days ago."

"I've been using those doors since I was basically a pup, Frostbite. They've never been a problem. But had we just used the doors, it would have been over so much faster. And the moment I knew you were stuck with me? Well, that was all the encouragement I needed to steal Bash's horses."

I drew backward. "You stole four horses from the Dark King?"

"I like to consider it 'borrowing without permission', but with every intention of returning if and when I can. Plus, it was technically five if you include the one I gave to the boy in River Coven. He'll get over it. He's really a pushover. Wait until you meet him."

Tucking myself into the crook of his arm, I laid an arm across his chest. "How did you find me?"

"Team effort. Raven handled the blizzard. She's kind of a badass with the right tools. Kir and Nym covered half the ground in beast form and Bash took to the skies. He spotted the corner of the tapestry you took from Enger's place. Speaking of which, I'm going to kill him. Just a fair warning."

"I had to sneak out," I lied. "He wouldn't let me leave."

He tapped the tip of my nose. "You're a shit liar."

"It's not his fault. He was not my keeper, Atlas. Had he refused to let me go, I would have found a way. It's what I do."

"I see," he said with a tone of finality that unsettled me. Lifting my arm, he ran a finger over the band around my wrist.

The marking of the spell that cursed me to do the goddess' bidding.

The deep chimes of a clock resonated down the long corridor outside the room. The first was faint, but as Solstice neared with each gong, a familiar feeling crept over me. It was the same every year.

Four.

Five.

I had eleven months of living my own life before the magic would consume me again.

Six.

Seven.

Eleven months until I'd have to force another soul into the hands of three Spirits with a proclivity for fear mongering.

Eight.

Nine.

The pressure and fear of restarting the cycle stole my breath.

Ten.

Eleven.

"Happy Solstice, Frostbite."

On the stroke of midnight, as Atlas' fingers brushed that marking, it vanished.

21

I blinked slowly, ignoring the ringing in my ears as his words settled within me. "I don't understand."

Atlas stood, crossing the room to reach into the pocket of his coat, hanging over the back of a chair. "You gave me my freedom, Marley. And not from the magic cursed upon you. But in the moments between. I thought I might return the favor."

He held his palm out to show me what he'd kept in his pocket.

"A saltshaker?"

"I never leave home without it."

I rubbed my fingers over my blank wrist.

"After you left, Future and I were standing over my grave. I closed my eyes, waiting for the memories to be gone. The last thing I saw was your face before she laughed. Which is the creepiest sound you'll ever hear in your life, by the way. And while she prattled on about the intention of magic and whatever other nonsense, I circled her, listening as I trapped her within a salt circle. Apparently, that's frowned upon."

I bit my lip, holding back my smile as I tried to imagine it. "Yes, I can see why."

He set the salt on the small table by the chair and came back to sit on the edge of the bed. "She screamed pretty loud and cursed me seven ways to Sunday. When that didn't work… I can be stubborn, you know. She called her sisters or whoever they are."

"Oh, shit."

"It gets better, I promise. So, the other two appeared directly beside her. Thus, trapping themselves in the salt circle as well. Apparently, Spirits will do anything for freedom, including making demands of a goddess. Which sounds like a ghosty if you ask me, but—"

His words were cut short as a floating drop of light fell from the ceiling and burst through the room, filling every nook and cranny and suspending time. An ethereal being, bright and pure, appeared, though I could not see her face through the luminescence of her form. I covered my eyes, listening as her echoed voice, as the purest sound I'd ever heard, rang free.

"My dearest girl," the goddess said, pushing so close to the edge of the bed, I wondered if Atlas would burn to pieces if she touched him. "The magic placed upon you was always meant to be a blessing not a burden. But some souls, the most empathetic of us, internalize and struggle far more than others."

She paused, and I considered dropping my hand from my eyes.

"You may look," she said as if reading my mind.

The edges of her figure wavered like a pool of water, though she was made of light and not liquid. I still could not see the perfect form of her face, but something within me knew the beauty without the fine details.

"The moment your brother was lost to you, your heart was marked. The burden of guilt you carried forced you away from those that you loved the most."

"Then why was I never a target for the Spirits?"

"You were, of course. Your journey was different, but your twin flame has found you. In healing his own mark, and in the sacrifice that he ultimately made, he has freed you both."

I sat straighter in the bed. "My twin flame?"

"Yes, Marley Stormborn. His soul has found you in every lifetime apart from this one, when yours found his. It wasn't his mark that drew you to him, it was your heart. And per my agreement with him, I bless you, and I set you free."

Searing pain seeped across my face as the light of her palm caressed me. Not enough to make me flinch, but enough to feel the burn of her blessing.

"Goodbye, Marley."

"Good—"

I couldn't finish before the light was gone.

Atlas leaped from the bed and spun in a circle, immediately scanning the room for danger. "What happened?"

With my palm still pressed to my cheek, I answered. "It was her. The goddess blessed me."

"Oh yeah. She likes to touch people. Apparently, it's—"

"Atlas?"

I rose from the bed to stand before him. "What did you sacrifice? She said your sacrifice saved me."

"It doesn't matter. I would have given everything." Moving so close there was no longer space between us, except a breath between lips, he continued. "There wasn't a thing she could have demanded that I wasn't willing to bargain for your freedom."

He grabbed my face, closing the space until his lips were on mine and we were moving backward, his hand burning a permanent mark on my body as he held me steady until we collided with the wall.

Hours later, we lay in the borrowed room in the castle, wrapped in silky sheets, naked, satiated, and falling more and more with each second that passed.

"Can I keep you forever?" he whispered, though I'd thought he'd fallen asleep.

"That sounds an awful lot like a commitment, Atlas," I answered, running a finger over his bare chest.

"Oh, good. I must have said it exactly right."

I didn't know what the future would hold for Atlas and me. I didn't even know if I'd ever tell him that he was my twin flame. My equal and my universal match. I didn't know a lot of things. But I knew this imperfect man was perfect for me, and even if we ran from the world, we'd at least have each other.

GLISTENING SNOW COVERED THE GROUND, BUT SOMEHOW, GIANT pillars of fire still circled the castle as the Solstice festivities began. I had a sneaking suspicion that it had something to do with the queen, but when I asked and Atlas only winked at me, I knew that was information I may never know.

With a warm drink in my hand, Atlas led me through the crowd until I finally caved and agreed to meet the king.

"Your grace," I said, swallowing my fear as I curtsied and shifted until I stood slightly behind Atlas. "Thank you for helping Atlas find me."

The king dipped his chin, the gold circlet on his head catching the last rays of winter sunlight. "It was my honor."

"This is just weird," Kirsi said, entering the circle we'd made in the crowd. "You don't have to bow to His *Too* Highness. It makes his head too big."

"Are you well?" Nym asked, resting her hands on my shoulders to search my face for discomfort. "You really should get her back inside, Atlas."

"I'm okay. Plenty warm, thanks to the queen's Solstice gift." I held out the tiny bracelet on my arm, showing off the little flame. It didn't burn but warmed me through.

"I'm glad they found you safely," a deep voice said from behind.

I whipped around to take in the larger-than-life man staring down at me.

"Tor this is Marley. Marley, you remember Torryn, right?"

"Have we met?" he asked, furrowing a brow. "Surely I would remember such a pretty face."

"Unofficially," I answered, unable to hide my blush as Atlas slid an arm around me.

"Back off, pretty boy. She's already taken. And I think someone's here to talk to you."

Andrew approached the friendly group, sliding his hat from his head as he looked at Atlas and then at Torryn. Atlas gave an encouraging head tilt toward Tor before frantically nodding.

"Atty said you wanted to see me?" the man asked, wringing his hat in his hands.

"I apologized to Andy here for keeping you the other night for work. I remember you saying how badly you felt, so I hope you don't mind, I invited him to join us."

"But I didn't—"

"Happy Solstice, buddy," Atlas said, clapping his friend on the back before pulling us away.

"Ha-happy…" His words were lost to the crowd as we let them have their space.

The moment we were alone, Atlas wrapped both arms around my shoulders and held me firmly to him as he sighed.

"I'm sorry I don't have a Solstice gift for you," I said, hugging him back.

"You saved me, too, Frostbite. Shared freedom."

A freedom I still did not know the true cost of.

"Atty!"

I would probably never get used to the Dark King standing

within a ten-mile radius of me. Never mind a few feet as he held a hand out to Atlas.

"I've been thinking about what we discussed earlier, and I want you to have this." He gestured over our shoulders, and we turned to see a man carrying something the size of a ship's wheel wrapped in brown paper. "It's for both of you."

"Aw, Bash." Atlas nudged me. "See? I told you he was a softy. You open it."

I peeled the wrapping as the man continued to hold the object, revealing what looked to be a giant, ornate gold mirror with delicate filigree around the edges. But when the mirror rippled, I drew my hand away in shock.

"What is it?"

"It's a door," Atlas said slowly.

"So that no matter where your journeys take you, my brother, you can always come home."

"I told Bash about trading between the covens, and if you want, he's going to help us build a route and trade agreements."

"Really?" I asked, turning toward the king, unsure if I wanted to hug him or cower.

"Whatever you need, Ms. Stormborn."

"Uh, about that. We might have to start with a horse."

The king's eyes narrowed on Atlas. "You mean my horse that you gave to the River Coven boy?"

Atlas flashed his famous crooked grin. "That's the one. Glad we could clear that up. What's that Tor?" He shouted over his shoulder, not in the direction of the giant man. "Be right there."

I HOPED I'D NEVER GET USED TO THE SOFT SOUNDS OF A MAN snoring beside me, a heavy arm around my waist as he dreamed.

Not because I didn't want it, but because I didn't want to forget how blessed I truly was.

As my eyelids grew heavy, sleep within a breath or two, the glow of something in the room startled me back to consciousness.

"Hello, witch."

I recognized the voice of Past but not the face she took. A small girl stared up at me. Icy blue eyes and bone straight, fire red hair. She couldn't have been older than ten.

"You were always my favorite little soul seeker. Did you know that?"

I tossed the blankets off me, sliding from under Atlas' arm as I slipped out of the bed and tied a robe around my waist.

"Why are you here? I thought I was free."

Her eerie voice echoed, though mine did not. "You are, but I have something to show you. Do you wish to know the sacrifice your lover made?"

She held out a tiny hand, tempting me to take it. I peeked over to make sure Atlas had not stirred awake.

"If he wanted me to know, he would have told me."

"That is not what I asked," she said, whipping across the room and snatching my arm.

The first time I'd witnessed a space around me change into another, it had been so unsettling, I'd nearly thrown up. Wrenching one's body into a memory was far more jarring than one could anticipate. But now, I hardly blinked. Until a scene I was not expecting unfolded before me.

"Hello, Marley." Past faded away, melting into the vacant face of Future.

But that was not what caused my heart to stop nor my breathing to cease. The room. The home. The faint smell of aged pears sitting in a bowl on a familiar counter.

"I'm sorry," I heard myself whisper from the door.

Every bone in my body wanted to melt as I fought the urge to collapse to the floor. No matter how urgently I wished to escape this moment, no matter how briefly I'd thought I'd won and the Spirits were behind me, I was stuck. Here. In the moment I'd dreaded since the day I'd walked out that door.

"Turn," Future demanded, her shadows creeping up frozen legs in warning.

I would do it on my own before I gave her that control.

Just inside the small door to their underground home, I glimpsed the backs of my parents, holding each other, weeping as they stared at me. Though my face held no color, Atlas stood behind me, quiet but there.

In seconds, they pulled me into their arms and held me, mumbling indecipherable words of forgiveness and love. I watched for only seconds before the room faded to black.

"They will forgive you if you can release the fear in your heart, or they will become marked. Your father is already fading."

I whipped around to protest, to beg for them, but she was gone. This was my choice and Future's promise. I would go immediately. There was solace in knowing the outcome. Knowing that Atlas would remain behind me, ever steady, regardless of my weakness. Maybe I couldn't save them from the past, but I would save their future.

"That's a wise choice," Past said, appearing once more. "And now for what I promised."

The goddess, though not as bright as my recent experience, hovered in an empty space with Atlas on his knees before her, head bowed.

"I am here to bargain for Marley's freedom."

The goddess huffed a laugh. "For one to be freed, one must be bound. The only bound souls I see here belong to my Spirits, Atlas Firepelt. Why have you trapped my beings?"

"She is bound. Your magic is a curse."

He finally lifted his head to look up at the goddess, but I turned my back.

"I do not wish to see this," I hissed to the little girl beside me.

"I know," she smiled, the sentiment so eerie, it raised the flesh on my arms.

The room swiveled as I was forced back around.

"I like Marley," the goddess answered. "I believe I will keep her."

The growl from Atlas was hardly human as he moved to his feet, never giving the goddess an inch. "Then I will keep your Spirits bound in that salt circle, and I will wait here for eternity. I'll die at your feet before I touch a grain of that salt."

"I am quite capable of moving the salt." The confidence in the goddess' voice was far less convincing than Atlas'.

"Then prove it," he said, voice low and drawn out. A dare if ever I'd heard one.

"What if I gave you back your wolf instead? Reversed the effects of the Book of Omnia. Would you let me keep her?"

A breath caught in my throat. I saw the look of longing deep within his eyes. The note of hesitation as he weighed and considered her words. But I did not fear his answer. Not as I knew he slept beside me. Instead, I only felt sad, realizing what he'd given up.

"Marley's freedom or nothing. I will not bargain. Especially for something I can live without."

"Your heart is good, Atlas." She lifted a hand to his cheek. "I bless you. And as such, at the stroke of midnight on Solstice, I will grant your twin flame her freedom. But then her soul and her heart are yours to protect."

"With my life," he answered as the room faded away.

"See you in a few years, Marley," the little girl said before she, too, vanished.

I stood stunned in the dark room, the man that had saved me sleeping soundly. He'd chosen me. The goddess could not have tempted him with anything greater, and though the weight of that temptation had struck him soundly, the mark on my wrist had still vanished. He'd saved me. In so many ways.

I crawled back into bed, sliding under his arm, and leaning up to kiss his cheek. "Our daughter is going to be so beautiful."

"I know," he whispered, still half asleep as he pulled me closer. "I'm in so much trouble."

THE END

BONUS CHAPTER

ATLAS

She was fucking beautiful. Lying naked, stretched across the bed in our room, nothing but moonlight shining down on freckled skin. Every part of me ached to touch her, to hold her, to push myself inside of her until she made those stunning little noises before she came.

I reveled in the way her chest rose and fell with each rapid breath, the arch of her back, and the flush that spread across her body. My eyes traced the curve of her breasts, the gentle slope of her stomach, and the inviting space between her thighs.

I reached across the bed, trailing a finger down her abdomen. Bumps rose at my touch, her body already responding to me, as it had from the first time I'd seen her. She'd reached into my chest and squeezed so relentlessly from day one, a truth I may never tell another soul. I was not weak. I was not one to succumb. But for her, I was anything and everything she wanted and needed me to be.

She rolled, hair fanning across the pillow as she opened

sleepy eyes to share a languid smile. "I love it when you wake me in the middle of the night."

I planted a hand on her ass. "You're such a beautiful liar."

She giggled, shaking the bed with laughter, wrenching my damn heart like she always did. I crept over her naked body, pinning her between my arms as I stared down into a face I'd never get enough of.

"Tell me again," I whispered, rubbing my nose on hers.

Her eyes searched mine as they lit with joy. "I love you."

I buried my hesitation into a deep dark place within me. "I love you too, Frostbite."

I did love Marley. I needed her like I needed to breathe. That constant ache when she wasn't tucked into my side was enough to end me. But there was a thorn. A small piece of me that would always stroke the fear of my past.

My fingers grazed the soft skin of her inner thighs, trailing a path of fire as I inched closer to her core. She squirmed beneath my touch, aching for more. Leaning down, my breath ghosted over her sensitive flesh, eliciting a shudder that ran through her body. I kissed her thighs, nibbled at her hip bones, and dipped my tongue into her navel, savoring every inch of her.

She looked away, lifting off the bed, nearly begging for more.

"Marley," I growled. We'd played this game enough for her to know exactly what I needed.

She turned her head, her eyes locking with mine, a mix of longing and surrender in her gaze. A sultry smile curved her lips as she obeyed, awaiting my next move.

"Good girl," I purred, the words dripping with a mixture of praise and control. The power surged within me, feeding a primal desire that consumed me.

I dragged my tongue up her slit.

"Please," she whimpered, her voice a desperate plea that fueled my own hunger.

With one swift motion, I buried my face between her thighs,

licking her, devouring her with a primal hunger. She tasted so fucking good. Like freshly picked fruit coated in honey. My own personal addiction. Her body trembled, her moans filling the room, hardening every inch of me. I watched as she gripped the sheets, her hips undulating in rhythm with my unrelenting exploration. Her fingers tangled in my hair, her grip alternating between gentle caresses and firm tugs, urging me on.

Release burst through her, a symphony of euphoria that played out before my eyes. I relished in the sight, in the way her muscles tensed and convulsed, in the way her breath hitched and her body moved, a dance of dominance and submission.

I positioned myself above her. My voice, husky and commanding, filled the room. "Eyes on me."

She obeyed beautifully. Exactly how I needed her. I set a relentless pace, each thrust bringing us closer to the edge. I got lost in those tiny little whimpers that would end me one day, watching as the carnal pleasure etched itself on Marley's face, her eyes glazed with a mix of ecstasy and surrender.

Time ceased to exist as we delved deeper into oblivion, uncovering new sensitive places and intimate secrets that only two souls deeply in love could. Our bodies molded together, tracing every curve and crevice, leaving no inch untouched.

The room became a sanctuary, a sacred space where our desires and fantasies intertwined. Whispers of adoration and rapture filled the air, punctuated by gasps and moans of ecstasy.

With one final thrust, burying myself as deep as I could as she clenched, I succumbed to the overpowering pressure, my release crashing through me like a tidal wave. The sensations reverberated through my body, leaving me breathless and sated.

Collapsing beside Marley, we lay intertwined, our bodies glistening with sweat. The room filled with a profound silence, accompanied only by the rhythmic beat of our hearts, a testament to the intensity of our union.

I laid there, twisting her hair between my fingers until her breathing slowed. Until she drifted back to sleep as if I'd never awoken her for selfish pleasure. That tiny hesitation I'd tried to bury crept forward in the full moonlight. An insatiable torture, no matter my attempts at avoidance. I couldn't help thinking that she was too good. Too perfect. And I was not enough.

Despite the fact I'd outsmarted the goddess' spirits and won her freedom a year ago, despite the fact that I'd bought a ring today, that edge remained. A dangerous cliff I was wary to tip over. I could not love Marley as thoroughly as she deserved and no matter how much I tried to hide that searing feeling, it'd embedded itself like a thorn in my heart. Because she was not immortal. I could not protect her from everything. She could still die, and I wouldn't live through that loss again.

Fear was a terrible beast.

A beast Marley knew as intimately as I did. One she'd battled the day she'd finally seen her parents again. I don't think her smile had ever shone so bright and beautiful. The forgiveness, understanding, and compassion from her parents was a balm she'd needed as much as I did. That closure from her past, the promise of a future with them, had released the permanent tension in her shoulders. The wrinkle in her brow. She'd held my hand tightly when they wept at the door. They'd hugged her and sobbed and everything that felt broken in our world, healed.

Except this one thing. The knowledge that she was fragile. Breakable, even when she was strong. And maybe I wouldn't be enough to save her from whatever battles we might face.

The unease built in my chest until I couldn't rub it away. I crept from the bed, moving to the window to stare at the full moon that called to me, dragging the dormant wolf from within my soul until he stalked deep within me, pacing as if preparing for a battle that wasn't really there.

The wolf seemed to howl, rattling me to my core. A sound I hadn't heard in so long now. I closed my eyes to the lament, letting it melt over me. Letting the ache in my heart from missing the wolf consume me. I'd accepted myself as a witch, but I missed the animal desperately. More than I'd ever speak aloud.

The second howl was jarring. A familiar call. Not from within but beyond. Standing outside the castle, twists of icy snow coating long hairs of fur, stood a lone white wolf. Powerful eyes staring directly into mine. Summoning me.

I staggered backward.

It couldn't be

I dressed as silently as possible, stumbling over the buttons and snatching my coat as I ran out the door, down the twisted halls of Bastian's castle, and to the snow-covered gardens. I approached carefully, warily.

A small growl left her throat, a wolf's prayer.

Falling to my knees before my mother, she stalked forward. I bowed my head, willing my heart to fucking beat. To feel the moment I'd dreamed of since the day she'd been taken from me. Pressing our heads together, her as a wolf and me, no more than a man, the terrible claws of regret threatened to shred me to pieces.

"I should have gone back for you. I should have fought him."

She spoke no words, did not move at all. For a moment, I wondered if this was merely a dream. A conjuring of my own heart. But though I held my eyes shut, grasping at her essence, I knew the moment she shifted, sitting on her knees before me.

"My sweet boy," she managed, lifting my chin with aged hands until I stared into eyes I thought I'd never see again. "That was never your journey. You are exactly who you are meant to be, living the life you were always supposed to live. Come." She rose from the ground, though she was so much smaller than I remembered.

I took her outstretched hand and let her lead me through ankle deep snow between the paths of frozen bushes.

"Tell me about your life, Mother. Tell me you're safe and happy."

She looked up at me over her shoulder with a gentle smile. "I am." She took several more steps, lingering as she did when deep in thought. "You are to marry soon, are you not?"

I jerked at her question. "How could you know that?"

I hadn't told a soul. Hadn't even been brave enough to ask Marley because of that fucking thorn.

"It doesn't matter how I know, only that I do."

I scratched my head, letting her hand fall away as I considered her words. Staring at her carefully, I noted the subtle differences between her aged face and the woman from my memories. The way the wrinkles gathered, the coarse, wiry hair with no shine. The way her smile didn't quite light her eyes the way it used to.

"Why now? After all of these years, why on the day that I bought the ring have you come?"

"Because Marley is your pack now. You cannot challenge for alpha. You are one."

"I've been the alpha of my own pack since the day I was thrown out of your home. I had a pack long before Marley showed up."

There was a challenge in her eyes. A glint I'd never seen before. She'd come here with a purpose, and she would see it through.

"Yet something is wrong," she said, pushing me to speak words I didn't want to say.

The world stopped as the truth sat heavily on my tongue. "I am not enough."

"Oh, Atlas. Of course you are."

I broke beneath my mother's gaze. "I cannot protect her from all the dangers of this world. I'll never be strong enough. And if I lose her, I won't survive it."

She moved in, putting those cold, wrinkled hands on both sides of my cheeks. "The way you feel is normal. The fear is only a healthy dose. There's trauma in your past, but you have the promise of a future. Be afraid, Atlas, but don't be consumed by it. Don't forget to live because of it."

"I'm not... I'm not afraid."

Pointing a tiny finger directly into my chest until it hurt, she scolded me. "You are afraid. And you should be. If you weren't, then you don't love her enough. Do you think your father threw you out of our house to be a monster? He thought he was saving me from a life where a son or a husband died. He thought you would challenge him the second you could. It wasn't an easy choice. It wasn't right, but it was a choice made out of fear."

"But he was wrong," I barked.

"Yes, well, Son. No one is perfect, least of all your father, may he rest in peace."

"He can rot, for all I care."

She shook her head. "I know your heart, Atlas. You don't mean that."

I lowered my voice. "Do you really?"

"More than you know, my boy."

I turned away, tilting my head up to the giant moon, letting it wash over me. Letting it soothe an ache.

"I've missed you for so long, and you're telling me you've always been right here?"

She joined my side, taking my hand. "Nearly always. The human lands stole you away for a while, but I waited and listened and dreamed of the day I'd see you again. You've grown up, Son. Perhaps in spite of us all."

"Not you, Mother. Never in spite of you." I peered down to look into that face one final time as a great wolf's howl pierced the night.

She shifted without another word, and I stood for hours, it seemed, watching the spot she'd vanished in the distant tree line. She'd left on her own accord this time. But it didn't hurt. It felt more like closure than anything I'd ever had, wrapped in those horrible memories of abandonment. But she was right. If I loved

Marley fearlessly, it would have been too easy. I needed to embrace the fear. And for her, I'd do it every fucking day for the rest of my life.

A lesson I would have to thank Past for, if she ever appeared as my mother again.

ACKNOWLEDGMENTS

I'll always stop to thank you, the reader, first. We've come so far with this story, and while I'm sad to leave this world behind, I'm so very happy with where it landed and even more excited for what's to come. Stay tuned for a sneak peek into the first chapter of my next book!

I want to take this opportunity to tell you a little story. Three months before the first book in this duology released, I sent a message to a friend, and I poured my heart out. I'd been doing every single thing I could think of to find success in publishing, and the sales were dead in the water (that's maybe exaggerating but stay with me). She'd told me… your next book is going to sell a million copies. Be patient. And so, I manifested all the success coming to me. Daily, I told myself: *it'll blow your mind. Be patient.* So, when The Unmarked Witch hit rankings I'd never seen… when it held those spots and people started talking and my notifications were going wild, I cried. I crumbled. I thanked every lucky star from here to the end of the universe because my dreams came true. And they continue to do so. I really wanted to write this story, just to have the opportunity to thank every reader, one more time. Every review matters. Every mention. Every interaction with things you see on social media, even every pre-order. From the bottom of my heart, thank you. I really hope you'll stick around.

This next book, a gothic fantasy romance with enemies to lovers, knife to throat, slow burn, found family, burn the world down for you tropes is going to be something so special. I can already feel it writing these first pages.

To my reimagined team, Meg and Darby, gah… I'm so grateful for both of you. You took time, even when you had your own deadlines, and held my hand through this story. You wrote with me, you pushed me, you inspired me, and you continue to do so. I'm so very grateful for you both.

To Tristopher, the lady that gets all the credit for inspiring me to follow a lifelong dream… I love you, friend. Thank you for being that person that told me to be patient.

To my husband, your incredible support now and always will drive me more than anything else in life. I know I get lost in my own world when I'm writing and I pace the kitchen and forget important things because I'm distracted, but you've always been a trooper and just let me follow every wild dream into oblivion. I've never been one to give up, but then you've never been one to let me either. You're pretty great, lover pants. (I hope everyone at your work reads this and teases you to the end of time.)

To Haley and Emma, stop growing up. It sucks. Just like… move back in and stay forever. We can build a compound. It'll be fun and not creepy, and you'll never get annoyed with me. I promise.

To Kylie, the one I get to keep a little while longer, middle school is hard, kid. Teenage girls are ruthless, and you've never batted an eyelash. You're stronger than you know, and I'm so proud of you. You can stay in the compound, too. Tell your sisters.

To my high school bestie, Jess. Girl… look at us now. I'll never forget the night I laid in my bed, texting with you at one am, swooning over Fen and daydreaming about the things that are happening around me right now. Thank you for reading every word multiple times, for proofreading and swooning and never once wavering in your love and friendship and encouragement. You inspire me always.

To Courtenay, my little book painter, Miss Simply Painted Pages, the world needs more people like you. Every time I see you in my DM's, I know I'm going to laugh. You're a little ray of smartass sunshine, and I think I'll keep you. Thanks for making the most beautiful custom edges for The Unmarked series.

To my ARC team and Tamantha and Lauren, the fearless leaders, thank you for helping me shout about this book way earlier than Christmas time. I've been so blessed with such an amazing group of women building me up and doing loads of marketing, and I'm so grateful.

To Jes and Britt, my TikTok dream team, I cannot thank you enough for being champions of my books from day one. There's not a single ounce of success with this story that I don't credit both of you for. I'll never have enough thank you's. Social media is a beast, and you're both doing incredible things for authors like me. Thank you for saying yes. Thank you for continuing to support me. Thank you for letting me crash into your DM's with things that aren't even book related because somewhere along the line, we forged friendships that matter. You're helping change lives. Don't ever let yourselves forget that.

COMING 2024

TIL DEATH

CHAPTER ONE

TIL DEATH

I'd sliced a blade across so many throats, if not for my diligent tracking, I couldn't give a number.

Three hundred and seventy-four.

I knew two facts. One: a gasp, no matter the state of the victim, would always follow it. They may sputter or gag on the blood filling their esophagus, but still, they gasp. And two: they won't die unless I'm the one holding the blade.

Until today, I didn't know it was possible for a person to smell worse than the sodden alleyway behind Lady Visha's brothel. Something putrid wafting off Death's appointed target had proven me wrong. It was either him or the blonde prostitute hanging off his good arm. But based on his stumble and the perfect cadence of her gloriously high heels, he was a good bet for the lack of hygiene. Her patron must have paid very well. Even though he didn't have a pot to piss in. That, or she'd found herself in severe debt to Lady Visha.

I didn't need to lean over the wrought-iron railing circling the rooftop to see where they were going, nor rely on Death's magic to guide me. Thomas Vanhutes had been the object of my obsession for weeks. Since the day after Death delivered his name, I knew where he lived and where he found pleasure. He slept on a stained mattress older than he was with no linens, and his crumbling apartment boasted a leaky faucet. Not surprising for someone living on Beggar's Row. At least he had shelter, which was more than most in that district. Including the giant black crows that hounded the vagrants. They were always watching. Perth's most notorious plague.

I leaped from the rooftop, avoiding the puddles that inundated the narrow alleyway like an incurable illness, clinging to the shadows along the close brick buildings. Crossing the uneven brick road to stay close to Thomas, I quickly scaled the next building, digging into the dilapidated edifice I'd grown so familiar with. Most dwellers of the twin kingdoms could navigate these roads in pitch black. The water reflected enough of the street lamp's cool glow to guide the way.

The birds pecking at the gaps between the bricks scattered when Thomas stumbled through. And, though he wobbled and his company clacked, I was as silent as the deaths I delivered. A weapon. Honed and sheathed for as long as I could resist the magic.

A woman's faint pants echoed through the next alleyway until she grew to a fake climax, satisfying her third patron of the night. The red-haired woman had perfected those moans, and Lady Visha had likely become even more wealthy because of it. As I passed, she held her breath. As if she'd felt me from above, Death's Maiden, like a promise of deliverance from her plight. There was hope in that breath. A wish, though she'd never know I was there, having perfected my stalking by the age of thirteen. Some miserable souls were just more desperate than others.

I crept away, eyes focused once more. She'd wipe the remnants of that man from between her legs with a dirty rag and move on to the next within the hour. There was no saving her. Though that was not my job. The twin kingdoms were full of dark merchants, crime lords, thieves, and brothels. Every person needed to be rescued from something, even the Perth king's daughter. I'd sooner fall under the thumb of The Maestro than endeavor to save the world.

I stalked him from the apartment rooftops, crouching and watching my victim carry on, his silhouette elongating as he neared his favorite alehouse. Every third night, he stopped at the Badger Hole for one final nightcap, and I preferred to avoid the street rats that swarmed outside.

He hesitated for only a second before letting the prostitute tug on his good arm, probably eager to end her suffering. Like most dwellers of Beggar's Row, she didn't flinch at the rodents. They were more welcomed in this city than the failing king.

Heel to toe, I paced along the adjacent rooftop, placating the magic with my movements; not to grant Thomas a final tupping before his ultimate demise, but to give the woman time to pay her debt. A mercy for him, perhaps.

The door would squeak if I opened it. Lifting or pressing down on the handle wouldn't stop the squeal, so I opted for the window. The bars had rusted away long ago, and I fit easily. Aside from the sniffling, the space was eerily quiet. The prostitute had never left, but I wasn't expecting to find her naked, gagged, and tied on her back to the kitchen table.

The leaky faucet dripped to a puddle on the piss-stained floor, and the woman lay spread open with Thomas passed out in the corner. He'd had far bigger plans than his drunken stupor would allow. As I neared him, the visions began. Death's magic showed me all the ways I could kill this man. Breaking every bone in his body until his tortured screams were no longer audible. Slicing him from nose to navel, letting his innards slink to the floor, leaving him to drown in his own blood.

Hand gripping the knife strapped to my waist, I fought the power that would eventually win long enough to free the whimpering woman. She rolled away with a groan before scrambling until her back hit the wall as realization sank in. My presence in the dead of night meant only one thing.

"Deyanira." The chokehold of shock rippled over her trembling features.

I didn't begrudge her for neglecting to use my title. Folding my arms across my chest, I let the sapphire blade of my curved knife show. "Is the debt paid?"

She held an arm up to count the red bands before nodding.

"You can stay and watch, but he'll be here in five minutes."

Dull brown eyes rimmed in smeared mascara widened, followed by the first authentic gasp of the night. She didn't say another word, only grabbed her clothes and hurried naked out of the apartment, the squeal of the door, the final goodbye.

"I don't blame you," I managed, unable to fight the magic any longer.

A single slice and the second gasp, the one I'd anticipated, satisfied the power throbbing through my body. *A name given, a body delivered.* That was my true role. That of a harbinger. A lone assassin in a world of none. Death's Maiden.

The gargle was hardly audible over the sound of the shrill ringing in my ears, the eerie retraction of magic leaving traces behind, reminding me I was still human, though every kill carried me one step closer to Death's Court.

Three hundred and seventy-five.

Sliding the only chair from the table, I sat, thrumming gloved fingers along the surface, waiting. Each second was a heartbeat. Each of Thomas' slowing rasps, a promise. I no longer watched the final rise and fall of a chest cavity. Though the first had conjured tears, by the fiftieth, my heart had turned to stone. The Gods had abandoned us to Death's ultimate reign, and this was the world he reaped. And me, his weapon.

Death came without ceremony this time. His shrouded figure, no more than an ominous mystery until he swept his shadowed hood back, revealing the face of a beautiful monster.

The most stunning man one may ever see, his immortal, god-like features every bit the trap. Jet black hair and a perfectly angular face only set the tone for those obsidian eyes.

"My darling," he purred as I bowed low. "You have never been a disappointment, Deyanira."

His voice was the sound a throat coated in warm, golden honey might be, but I knew better than to utter words in his presence, especially when he tucked a finger under my chin, pulling me from the rancid floor while I watched the name burned into my palm wither away to embers and ash.

Death pressed cool lips to my cheek as he did with every meeting. Floating above my victim, he drew Thomas' soul from his body, eyes glistening with mirth before he laughed and dragged him off to his eternal court.

Want more? Be sure to follow Miranda on your favorite social media or check out her website.

Instagram, TikTok, Facebook, Amazon
www.authormirandalyn.com

www.ingramcontent.com/pod-product-compliance
Lightning Source LLC
Chambersburg PA
CBHW020503310726
48979CB00016B/2763/J

* 9 7 9 8 9 8 8 0 7 0 7 1 9 *